The Cradle Will Fall
Samantha Baca

Haven Brook Series

'Til Death Do Us Part

The Cradle Will Fall

The Ties That Bind

A Very Haven Christmas

Three Strikes, You're Gone

Contents

Contents

<u>One</u>
Noah

"Just put the knife down, please. You don't want to hurt her." My voice was unusually calm and steady given how I felt anything but calm. My eyes darted around the room, following her every movement as she placed the tip of the knife under Jade's throat while pulling her hair to keep her head tilted back. I swallowed hard, desperate for a way to get in between her and Jade. One quick movement could be fatal for Jade, so I had to stay calm. Her life depended on it.

I tried to lean forward slightly without drawing too much attention. If she would just step out of the shadows, I could see her face and know who I was dealing with. My hands felt sweaty as I ran them down the front of my jeans, making sure I was ready for whatever might happen.

"You don't know what I want," she rasped, her voice barely above a whisper. She shifted in the darkness, taking a step backward with Jade still in her grip.

"Don't take her, please, just let her go," I pleaded as they slipped further into the shadows. Within seconds I no longer saw Jade's face. I reached out to grab her as the knife swung out and sliced my wrist. I watched as the blood ran down my hand and puddled by my feet, the life in me slipping away into the same darkness.

"If you really love her, then you must die for her." Her voice floated above me as I stumbled further into the darkness until it was pitch black around me. Jade was gone and within seconds, so was I.

I sprung forward in bed, gasping for air the way I always did when I had one of these dreams. They were almost predictable at this point and began soon after Jade and I had started seeing each other again. It seemed the closer we got, the more often the dreams would come. Almost like some sort of bad omen for us to be together and settle down.

I glanced down beside me; Jade's hair was fanned out across her pillow as she slept. She had changed so much since the day I first met her, the short black hair with red streaks through it was now blonde and almost touched her ass. While I loved the black hair, I was digging the blonde these days. That was Jade though, always keeping me on my toes, as wild and unpredictable as they come.

I reached down and gently pulled the blanket up over her back, the room a little more chilly than normal with the recent storm that had rolled through. Winters in Colorado could be rather brutal, and this year was starting out to be a tough one. Usually, I would have adjusted the temperature before going to bed but we had been a little busy and needless to say, hadn't noticed the cold.

I glanced over at the alarm clock beside my bed, groaning silently when I saw it was already five in the morning. I could either lay in bed and toss and turn for another hour until Jade and I had to get up for work, or I could just give in and get up. Reluctantly I rolled over and slid out of bed, careful not to wake her up.

The hardwood floors were cold beneath my bare feet as I walked down the hallway and turned up the heater. I programmed the coffee maker for 6:30 and made my way to the guest room that I had recently been using as a workout room. It's a funny thing when you get involved in a committed relationship, suddenly you need different ways to burn off some stress when you don't sleep with random women anymore.

An hour later and I was finishing my kettlebell routine when I saw Jade lean against the doorway, hair still tousled, wearing nothing but one of my worn-out T-shirts that barely covered her ass. I sucked in a deep breath, her beauty constantly taking my breath away.

"You're up early again, everything okay?" She walked over and sat on the bed against the wall and looked at me, concern filling her emerald green eyes.

"Yeah, just couldn't sleep." I shrugged as I opened the closet door and put the kettlebells away. The room was barely big enough to function as a guest room without having the constant clutter of my expanding collection of workout gear.

"Another bad dream?" She tilted her head to the side and watched me. I let out a deep breath and went to sit by her on the bed. She leaned into my chest as I wrapped an arm around her and held her.

"Yeah."

"Do you want to talk about it?" I could hear the tiniest bit of hope in her voice, each time she asked it was less and less with each time I said no. There was no way that I could bring myself to talk to her about the nightmares I was having about someone trying to kill her.

"Nope. But thanks." I squeezed her shoulder gently and planted a kiss on her forehead.

"Well, in that case, I'm going to jump in the shower. I can't afford to be late today, we have a new teller that I've been assigned to train so I have to make a good impression." She hopped off the bed and lingered for a moment in the doorway, looking back at me over her shoulder. "But I do have a few minutes to spare if you wanna join me."

I saw the look in her eye and jumped off the bed, chasing her down the hallway as she squealed and ran ahead. Within seconds my T-shirt was pulled over her head and flung backward at me as she kept running the short distance to the shower, her bare ass and butterfly tattoo greeting me as I caught up to her. My hand reached out and grabbed her before she slipped away and darted into the shower. The hot water started to fog up the glass of the shower door, her eyes watching me as the water ran down her body. It was like a game of cat and mouse and I never got tired of playing it with her. Jade was carefree and playful, and it was one of the things that drew me to her the most. That and her ass.

What was supposed to be a quick shower turned into a long, cold one as the hot water ran out by the time we were ready to actually shower. I let Jade finish up first so she could have the last of the warm water while I took a much-needed cold shower. Being with Jade was pretty much the equivalent of being on Viagra, she could keep me going for hours.

I was in the kitchen pouring our coffee into travel mugs when she walked in wearing a black and white polka dot skirt with a black silk shirt. It was always such a mind fuck for me to see her get dressed up for work, looking professional, and completely put together when I got to see the wild side as soon as she got home. I couldn't lie, it also made for some freaking hot role-playing in the bedroom.

"You look nice, should I be jealous of this new hire?" I joked as I tightened the lid on her mug and handed it to her.

"Relax, it's a woman." She rolled her eyes as her heels clicked across the floor as she walked to the fridge and grabbed a yogurt for breakfast.

"Well... I've never been known to be one to complain...." I winked as she suggestively licked a spoonful of yogurt into her mouth.

"You're impossible." She shook her head and took another bite.

"A guy could fantasize."

"Oh really? So that's your fantasy? Me with another woman?"

"Well, I would be there too, of course." I shot her a playful look as she rolled her eyes again, a smile spreading across her face.

"So you, me, and Cindy Belmont." She ate her last bite of yogurt and sat the spoon in the sink. "I can always ask if she's interested while I'm training her. Just gotta pick the right time. Maybe after money laundering but before armed robbery?" Her eyes danced wildly as they watched mine as she toyed with the idea, teasing me every step of the way.

"Wait- what did you say her name was?" I heard her say it the first time but there was no way that she had actually said that name. My stomach felt uneasy as I waited for her to confirm.

"Cindy Belmont." She tilted her head to the side as she walked past me to throw her empty container away. "Why, do you know her?"

I swallowed hard and tried to think of how to answer that. Did I know her? No. Did I fuck her? Yes. She was a one-night stand that I had the night that Jade and I got into a fight and called it quits. That was six months ago, right after Chase and Mia's wedding and I hadn't seen or heard anything from Cindy since it happened. There was no fucking way that the woman I slept with from a one-night stand was the same woman who was now going to be working with my girlfriend, was there? I cleared my throat and walked past her to the sink, desperate to hide the look on my face.

"Doesn't sound familiar, no."

"Well, I guess I should go or I'm really going to be late."

"Okay, text me on your break." I smiled as I felt her arms slide around my waist and hug me from behind.

"Are you feeling okay?"

"Yeah, I'm fine. Why?" My heart was racing as I was anxious to get away from her long enough to find out whether or not the Cindy she was going to be working with was the same Cindy I had slept with. While it shouldn't have been an issue given that we had broken up, I hadn't been honest with her about whether I was with anyone else when she asked me about it when we got back together.

"Because you didn't follow that sentence with your usual, 'send me some nudes'." Her voice was low as she mocked me saying it.

"You know I never say no to those." I turned my head to smile at her as she stayed wrapped around my back.

"And you know I don't take them." She swatted my ass then turned to walk away.

"I'll talk to you later," she called over her shoulder as she walked out the door.

"Sounds good."

The door closed, leaving me running late for work and distracted with a problem I didn't want to have to deal with.

Two
Noah

"You're in early for a Monday." Chase leaned against the doorway and crossed his arms over his chest.

"I'm surprised you're here at all, isn't Mia supposed to pop any day now?" I kept my attention on my computer and didn't bother to look up to make small talk. There was too much on my mind and I needed to clear it before I had to go upfront and be around other people in a few hours.

"Any day now." He ran a hand down the scruff on his face, evidence that he hadn't taken the time to shave this week.

"So what are you doing here? Shouldn't you be at home helping her practice her breathing or something?" My brow furrowed as I stared at my computer, not finding anything on Cindy. I didn't know why it was bothering me so much that she was back in town given that we had only had one night together, but something kept eating away at me as I thought about her working with Jade. Was this what it felt like to be with someone who finally made me worry about getting caught doing something that I knew I shouldn't have done?

"Practice her breathing? Really?" He pushed off the wall and walked around to my desk, looking over my shoulder at the computer.

"Who is Cindy Belmont?" He leaned down and peered at the computer screen to read the name and the very few Google results it came up with.

"No one." I pushed the keyboard away from me and leaned back in my chair as he took a step back and looked down at me.

"What's up Noah? And stop with the whiny bullshit, just tell me what's going on."

Chase and I had one of those love/hate brotherly relationships which worked out well given he had been my best friend since we were little and we now ran a brewpub together. We had the natural ability to call the other out on their shit and knew when something was going on, which unfortunately for me, meant that he knew something was going on.

"She's a new girl at the bank, Jade's training her today."

"Okay- so what's the problem? Why are you Googling her?" He pulled his brows together in confusion.

"I slept with her." I let out a heavy sigh as I finally said the words out loud to someone else.

"You cheated on Jade?" His tone was harsh as he stared at me, waiting for me to confess just how badly I fucked up.

"Yeah... No. I don't know?" My head was a mess as I had spent the last hour asking myself the same thing.

"How do you not know? If you slept with someone other than Jade, you cheated on her. It's pretty simple."

"What's pretty simple?"

I looked up to see Chase's younger brother Grant walk into the office and smile as he looked back and forth between the two of us.

"Noah isn't sure whether he cheated on Jade by sleeping with someone else," Chase explained as he leaned against the wall beside me, Grant sitting down in the chair in front of my desk.

"You cheated on Jade? Really bro? She's literally the perfect girl for you, why would you do that?"

I threw my hands up in exasperation and shook my head.

"I didn't cheat on Jade. I slept with someone else six months ago, when her and I had that huge fight and broke up. It was a one-night stand that meant nothing."

"Okay, then I'm confused- why are we talking about it?" Grant pulled his eyebrows together.

"We aren't." I leaned back against the cool leather of my high back chair and shut my eyes.

"So you slept with her while you guys were broken up, it was a one-night stand, and now she's working with Jade. Am I missing anything?" Chase looked over at me and waited for an answer.

"Jade asked me when we got back together if I had been with anyone else during the time we were broken up. I said no."

"Fuck." Chase exhaled and shook his head, realizing what the problem was.

"Double fuck." Grant leaned back in his chair and gave me a sympathetic half-smile.

"So now I don't know what to do because the girl I had a one-night stand with six months ago just mysteriously showed up in town and is working with my girlfriend. I mean, what am I supposed to do? Do I come clean and tell Jade before she possibly finds out, or do I just ignore it and pray that Cindy keeps her mouth shut and forgot about me completely?" I looked back and forth between them, hopeful that one of them would have a logical answer for me.

A few minutes of silence passed as they exchanged a few unsure glances before Chase finally spoke.

"I say don't tell her. What's the likelihood that she'll find out anyway? If this girl was interested in anything with you, she would have made a move back then. I don't think there's any reason to hurt Jade when you guys have come this far in your relationship."

"I agree, nothing good will come from telling her." Grant shrugged his shoulders before a smirk crossed his face. "And on a different subject, is Cindy cute?"

"Gross! You don't want Noah's sloppy seconds." Chase laughed as he pushed off the wall and pulled his phone out of his pocket.

"What?! It's a small town and Noah has slept with pretty much every girl here. It's literally impossible to find someone he hasn't slept with."

I tried to keep a straight face but failed as I joined Grant in laughing at how true that statement was. There really weren't that many girls in town that I hadn't already been with, but that's also because not many new people move here, and I started at an early age. I looked up at Chase as he stared blankly at his phone.

"You okay, Chase? You look like you just saw a ghost." I chuckled as I leaned forward and waited for him to snap out of the daze he was in.

"Yeah, I'm fine. Mia's water just broke." He slid the phone back into his pocket and looked at us as if nothing had happened.

"Are you just going to stand there or are you going to get your wife to the hospital?" Grant asked as he stood up and looked at Chase. A few seconds passed before Chase registered the words.

"Shit! It's time!" A look of panic crossed his face as he patted down his pockets for his car keys before spinning on his heel and running out the door. Grant and I exchanged a look before bursting into laughter.

"You laugh now, one day that'll be you, my friend."

"I don't know about that. Jade's not looking to settle down and we're taking it slow. Who knows what the future has in store for us?" I looked away and pretended to be doing something on my computer to take the focus off of me. Grant had always been like a little brother to me growing up and had the same annoying knack for reading me that Chase did.

"What do you want? Do you think someday you might want to get married and have kids?"

"Honestly, I don't know." I sighed and pushed back from the computer when I realized that Grant wasn't going anywhere nor was he going to let this conversation go. The problem was that I had thought a lot about my future lately and that probably scared me more than anything.

"It's okay to want more out of life. Sometimes I think about trying to meet someone new and seeing where it could go. I know Liam misses Renee and while I would never want to try to replace her, I think he would like to have a woman in our lives again. I can't give him back the mom he had, but that doesn't mean that he doesn't deserve to know that kind of love as he grows up." His eyes filled with tears as he looked away and my heart broke for him the same way it did the day Renee lost her battle to cancer.

It was coming up on the 3 year anniversary of her passing and Liam was starting to test his dad the way all ten-year-olds do. While I couldn't imagine trying to find love again after everything Grant went through, I knew him well enough to know that he was also looking out for his son. It was a delicate balance that Grant was constantly working to maintain as he did the best he could to raise his son on his own.

"Sometimes I think that I want that life." I sighed and looked down.

"What life is that?"

"The whole happily ever after. Getting married. Having kids. I see Chase and Mia together and they make it look so easy."

"They are good for each other and when you find someone like that, it does feel easy. Just like what you've found with Jade."

I looked up at him and saw the words written on his face that he didn't have the heart to say.

"I have to tell her what happened, don't I?"

He nodded his head in agreement as he gave me another half-smile. I let out a deep breath and leaned back. I knew it was only right to tell Jade what happened, she deserved to know if we were going to try to build a life together. But the thing that I feared the most was what she would say when she found out. Would she curse me out and be pissed at me then get over it? Or would she be the Jade that I knew and thank me for telling her the truth before walking out and leaving me forever? My heart clenched as I knew the answer.

"Well, on that note, I should get out of here before you need to get upfront to open." He stood up and pushed in the chair. "If you talk to Chase, let him know that I'll get the tool bag from him later."

"Did you need to borrow tools? I have mine out in the truck."

"If you don't mind, that would be great. I would just steal his but they're in his truck which is now gone." He laughed and waited while I leaned back and dug the keys out of my pocket before tossing them to him.

"Thanks, I'll bring them back this afternoon."

"Sounds good. I'm gonna head upfront, you can just leave my keys on the desk when you're done." I walked by and clapped him on the shoulder as we walked down the hallway together.

"You deserve to find love again, don't ever forget that."

"So do you, Noah. Let me know how it goes when you tell her." He chuckled softly as he walked away and for a moment, I felt like myself again.

I wasn't the guy who was romantic and thinking about love and starting a family. I was the guy who was constantly with a different girl and getting my balls chopped by the guys for my reckless behavior. I took a deep breath and prayed that the day would be busy so I could keep my mind off of the things I wasn't ready to deal with.

Three
Jade

It was mid-morning and I felt like I had been talking for hours in a one-sided conversation. It was rare that we ever had new hires at the bank, and this was the first one that I was responsible for training. I had expected it to be more of a question and answer type setting while she preferred a lecture instead which meant I had been the only one talking all morning. I constantly tried to engage her in the conversation and ask if she had any questions, but she was yet to interact with me.

"Okay, we've covered a lot. Why don't we take a 15 minute break then we'll get started again?" I smiled and picked up the pages of the training binder that we had already covered and moved them to a small pile on the corner of the desk.

"Thank you! This baby is sitting on my bladder, so I really need the bathroom." She stood up and out of nowhere a very pregnant belly greeted me.

"Of course. See you in 15 minutes." I smiled awkwardly as she walked off and made her way to the bathroom. She had on a loose shirt with a flowy skirt that hid her bump as she walked away but part of me wondered why I hadn't seen it before then.

I stood up and smoothed down the front of my skirt before walking to the break room to fill up my water bottle. It felt nice to stand up for a few minutes and stretch my legs. My body was sore from sitting idle for so long that I couldn't wait to get home and do some yoga. I thought about texting Mia to see if she would want to get together and do some light yoga with me when I saw Cindy come out of the bathroom and make her way toward the break room. I smiled as I walked past her, sitting my water bottle on my desk before heading to the bathroom.

The day felt long and tedious just sitting there and going over every single page of the training manual. I finished up and walked back to my desk, surprised to see her sitting there, waiting for me.

"Alright, I thought it might be a nice little break to take a few minutes to get to know each other before we jump back into the training. Is that alright with you?"

"Sure." She smiled meekly as she sat on her hands and crossed her ankles in front of her.

I took a deep breath and turned to face her, worried that this was going to be like talking to a wall. She was very quiet and didn't strike me as the kind of person who had a lot to say.

"So, are you new to Haven Brook?"

"Yeah, I just moved here."

"Oh yeah, where did you move from?"

"Eastern Point, it's about an hour away. My family still lives there."

"What made you want to move here?"

I hated small talk more than anything and here I was, trying to find something to talk about with this girl who looked like she'd rather do anything else in the world than sit here and talk to me. This is what good employees and trainers do, I reminded myself.

"Well, I kinda want to find this guy that lives here."

"Oh yeah?" I raised my eyebrows as I waited for her to tell me more.

"Yeah, we had a thing one night six months ago, and well, as you can see...." Her voice trailed off as she giggled and rubbed a hand over her stomach.

"Does he know that you're pregnant?" I smiled as she looked down adoringly at her stomach.

"Not yet. I didn't have his information when I left, it was all so quick before I had to go. But I know he grew up here so I don't think he would have left." She sighed heavily. "At least I hope not."

She reminded me of an innocent girl who fell in love for the first time and it brought a wave of happiness over me.

"I'm sure he's still around. What's he look like? Maybe I know him?" I leaned forward on my desk and watched her shift nervously across the desk from me as her eyes lit up with excitement.

"Oh my, well, he's gorgeous. Like really, really gorgeous. He has jet black hair and these really pretty eyes. They're kinda brown but also kinda green. It's weird, it's like they're two colors mixed into one."

"Hazel?" I tilted my head and watched her reaction as the word flowed off my tongue.

"Yes! That's it- they're hazel. Gosh, this baby is making me lose all of my smartness." She giggled and I smiled back, fighting the urge to tell her that wasn't a word.

"He sounds very good looking."

I watched as her eyes lit up and silently wondered just how many guys in Haven Brook fit that description, knowing the answer that I didn't want to accept. There was only one.

<u>Four</u>
Noah

"She is beautiful. Congratulations you guys." I stared down at the most beautiful teeny tiny baby wrapped up like a burrito with a handful of blankets. My heart felt so heavy and full that I had to blink several times to force the tears back.

"Hey guys, can I come in?"

My head lifted to the sound of Jade's voice as she quietly opened the door to Mia's hospital room.

"Get your butt in here and meet your niece!" Mia exclaimed excitedly. I looked over and caught a glimpse of the look her and Chase shared as they watched me hold their daughter.

"Oh my gosh!" Jade squealed quietly as she looked over my shoulder at the baby while washing her hands in the sink behind me. I laughed when I watched her struggle to stay focused on drying her hands as she rushed to hold the baby. A paper towel flew by my head, missing the trash can, as Jade reached her arms out in front of me for the baby.

"Can I help you?" I teased as I pulled the baby in closer to my chest. She raised an eyebrow while pursing her lips, a look I could never take seriously when she was mad because she was so damn cute.

"Wilder, if you know what is good for you, you'll hand over that baby," she warned playfully, reaching in to take her.

"Fine, but you have to sit first. You're too antsy, I'm not going to risk you hurting my niece." I slowly got up, clutching the baby to my chest to keep her safe. Never in my life had I ever held something so delicate and fragile.

"Alright, move out of my way." She smiled excitedly as she sat down and held her arms out for the baby. I gently leaned forward and waited until I could feel Jade's arms around her before I pulled back, still keeping my hands right under the baby just to be safe.

I watched as Jade's eyes lit up the moment she looked at her, taking my breath away. For a moment I imagined what she would look like seeing our baby for the first time. I shook my head to clear my mind of the image and kissed her forehead before stepping to the side of her to pick up the paper towel and throwing it in the trash.

"She's perfect. Absolutely perfect." She looked up at Mia with tears in her eyes as they shared a silent moment that lead to both of them crying. It was getting to be too much in this room, too heavy with all of the emotions flying around me.

"Thank you," Mia and Chase said at the same time, looking at each other and laughing afterward.

"Have you guys picked a name?" I asked, hoping to lighten the mood some. I watched as they looked at each other and Chase smiled at Mia as he nodded and smiled. Mia turned to us and sat up straight with a proud smile on her face.

"Guys, we would like to introduce you to Rylee Rose Walker." Her smile beamed across her face, Chase's arm wrapping tight around her shoulders as he placed a tender kiss on her cheek.

"I love it!" Jade looked down at the baby and gently rubbed her cheek with her finger. "Hello, Rylee Rose. I love you so much already, sweet girl."

"It's a beautiful name you guys."

"Thanks, we wanted something meaningful and Rylee means courageous. We changed the spelling to make it more unique, but we think it fits her already."

"It definitely fits her, Mia. She's going to be courageous just like her momma."

"Knock, knock. Is it safe to enter?" Grant's voice called out from behind the door and we all laughed at how no one felt safe entering the room of a new mother.

"Come on in, brother." Chase smiled as Grant and Liam came around the corner, a pink teddy bear in Liam's arms as he stayed close to Grant.

"Hey buddy, would you like to come in and meet your cousin?" Chase looked over at Liam and smiled as he slowly walked over to where Chase was sitting on the bed next to Mia.

Jade smiled sweetly as she slowly stood up and carried the baby over to Chase, giving Liam a few minutes to get situated on the couch next to the bed. Grant sat beside his son and I saw a look of pain on his face as his son reached out and carefully pulled the tiny baby close to his chest and rested her on the pillow they placed on his lap. I could never imagine what it felt like to be Grant, to start my life with someone who I planned to spend forever with only to have that pulled out from underneath me before it even got started. Everyone knew that Grant and Renee had wanted a big family, he wanted three kids, she wanted four. Seeing his son holding a newborn baby, knowing that he wouldn't have a sibling of his own had to kill Grant deep down inside.

The thoughts of Grant's life and what all he was missing out on flooded through my head and took me back to the same nagging questions that I had been having for months now. Was I ready to finally settle down and did I really want to get married? Were kids going to be part of my future? I had a wonderful childhood growing up but I've never felt like I was destined to be a dad, and quite frankly, I wasn't sure that I wanted to be one. But now something was different. I remembered the feeling of Rylee's tiny, delicate body in my hands, and all of a sudden, I wanted more than anything for Grant to find love again and have the family he dreamed of. And I wanted it for myself as well.

My heart started racing as I realized what was happening and suddenly, I wanted to get down on one knee and propose to Jade before running her home and knocking her up. The hospital had to have been putting some mind-altering drugs through the vents that made people delusional. That was the only explanation.

"You okay?" Grant looked over at me, breaking my attention with his question. My cheeks felt red and flushed, my throat suddenly dry.

"Yeah. I'm good."

"We should probably get going and give them some time with Rylee."
Jade nodded toward Grant and Liam as she picked up her purse and slung
the strap over her shoulder. She looked at me in a way I hadn't seen before
and for a moment, I could swear that she looked upset with me.

"That's a good plan, want to follow me home? We can go grab something
for dinner or I can order a pizza, just let me know what you prefer."

"Actually, I think I'm going to stay at my place tonight." Her lips were
pursed as her arms crossed across her chest. I had only seen this look
a handful of times, but I knew enough to know that this wasn't going
to end well. Why was she so upset with me? She seemed fine until she
came to meet the baby. Was it because we weren't moving forward
in our relationship and she was mad because she wanted a family and
thought that I didn't? A hundred questions came flooding through my
mind as I thought about what I should say with everyone watching us.

"Is everything okay?" I went with the safest response I could think of
on the fly.

"Yeah, I'm fine. I just need some space. I have a lot that I need to think about."

Shit. This was definitely about the baby. It had to be. I rolled my eyes
and took a deep breath as I silently cursed her for making me look like
a pansy in front of the guys but if she needed a big song and dance, I
would give it to her. Hell, she could ask for the moon and I would try
to find a way to get it for her.

"Look, Jade, I think there's something that we need to talk about."
I moved my eyes slowly to the door, hoping she would take the hint
and move our conversation to the hallway. If I was going to bare my
soul and look like a total pussy at least it would be in the presence of
doctors and nurses that were used to men wallowing in front of women
since this was the maternity ward.

"I think there is." Her lips were pulled in a tight line, her jaw set. The look
in her eye told me everything and I knew at that moment that this was no
longer about her wanting to have a baby. This was about Cindy. She knew.

I tried to brace myself for the slew of profanities I was sure were about
to come from her mouth but was surprised when she stayed quiet and
stared at me, waiting for me to talk. I wanted to come clean and tell her
about Cindy, I really did. But for whatever fucking reason, I wasn't able
to. I glanced over at Grant, my eyes pleading for him to give me some
sort of advice to help me through this as he subtly nodded his head.

"Jade….. I um….." I cleared my throat and tried to ignore everyone as they stared at us. "I think you should move in with me. Permanently." I blew out the breath that I was holding and saw Grant's head drop to his chest as he slowly shook his head no. Chase arched an eyebrow before looking away and quietly whispering something in Mia's ear.

"I don't think that's a good idea."

"Why not?" I knew that I didn't really want to know the answer but I asked anyway. It felt like it was impossible to avoid asking. It was like a band-aid that was wrapped too tightly around an oozing wound. You had to pull it knowing that it was going to hurt like hell every inch of the way.

"I think you know why." She shifted her weight and a sadness crossed her face. I swallowed hard as my heartbeat raced.

"Jade, please," I whispered.

"You should have told me. You should have told me when it happened and not let me accidentally find out. Did you think I was stupid?" Her brows pulled together as she glared at me.

I licked my lips and lowered my head, my eyes closed to avoid having to see the look on her face. When I opened them, she was gone.

Five
Jade

"You don't have to stay on the phone with me, you should get some rest or go snuggle that sweet girl of yours." I wiped my nose with the tissue that was falling apart from using it so much. I took a ragged deep breath and held my phone closer to my ear, desperate for the comfort that Mia was providing on the other end.

"Chase is snuggling Rylee so I have some downtime and honestly, I need something to distract myself for a little bit. I've been so consumed with the pregnancy and everything else that I feel like I don't even know what's going on around me. And I really want to know." Her voice was gentle as she said that last sentence and I felt myself starting to cry all over again.

"Jade, what happened? Talk to me."

"Do you remember that big fight that Noah and I had a while back? The one right after your wedding?"

"Yeah."

"Well, I asked him after we got back together if he had been with anyone else while we were broken up and he said no. He asked if I had been with anyone, and I said no." I took a moment to try to collect myself as I had been playing this over and over in my head since Cindy had told me about the guy she came here to be with. Mia stayed quiet as she waited for me to go on.

"I trusted him. Even though I knew deep down that I shouldn't. He's Noah- everyone wants him and he's always getting with a different girl. Why did I think that it would have been any different when we broke up for two weeks?"

"Did he tell you that he was with someone else?" She spoke softly and I wasn't sure if it was to try to help keep me calm or if it was to let Chase and the baby rest, but either way, I was thankful for it as it actually did calm me down some.

"No. But I'm 99.9% sure that he was with someone else."

"What would make you think that?"

"We have a new hire at work, a girl that just moved here from Eastern Point. She said that she moved her to find the guy she had a one-night stand with."

"Did she say that it was Noah? Because there are a lot of guys in Haven Brook that are known to have one-night stands. Chase's youngest brother, Wyatt just got himself into some trouble with the same thing." Mia sighed and I let out a soft laugh as I knew just how much trouble Wyatt was getting into as he was coming to Noah for help every other weekend.

"No, but she didn't have to. She described the guy as gorgeous with black hair and hazel eyes. How many guys do you know that look like that here?" My voice was laced with a little too much sarcasm and I hated myself for how jealous and insecure I sounded. Part of me wanted to just ask Noah about it and be a grown-up, mature person, but the other part of me felt so hurt and betrayed that I couldn't find it in me to be that.

"Well, that is pretty hard to say- yeah, I'm sure she was talking about someone else." Mia sighed as I heard her shushing in the background.

"Yeah, it definitely is." I shifted my weight on the couch and grabbed my wine glass from the table, taking a big sip, enjoying the feeling of the cold liquid as it ran down the back of my throat. "I can let you go, Mia, I don't want to keep you from your family."

"Oh, shush."

"Okay, I'm going to let you go. I'll talk to you in a few days, see how you guys are doing and if you need anything."

"I was shushing you, Jade."

I started laughing and could hear Mia join in on the other end.

"Okay, so let's go ahead and agree that Noah slept with another woman who has come back into town and wants to be with him. You don't know for sure that she slept with him when you guys were broken up, it might have been before you guys ever got together. Noah is completely in love with you, Jade. There's no way that he's going to leave you for some girl that he had a one-night stand with." Her voice was so positively reassuring that I didn't want to break the news to her.

"She's six months pregnant and came back to make things work with the baby's daddy." I closed my eyes and sunk lower into the couch as I brought my wine glass up and held the cold glass to my swollen eyes. I wasn't one to cry but for whatever reason, this really broke me. I couldn't figure out if I was more upset with Noah for not telling me about the other girl after it happened, or if it was because I knew that he would leave me to be with her. He may not love her but he would do the right thing.

"Oh my god." She let out a heavy breath leaving us both sitting in silence for a few minutes.

"What are you going to do?"

"What can I do? I can't be the person who stands in the way of a father being part of his child's life. I have to walk away." A sob escaped my throat before I could stop it.

"Oh, honey…. I wish I was there with you right now, you shouldn't have to go through this alone."

"Thanks, I'll be fine though. I just need to get out whatever it is that I'm feeling right now and then move on."

"Is it really that easy?"

"No. But when you truly love someone, sometimes you have to let them go. And as hard as it will be, I have to let him go, Mia. Maybe he was never mine to begin with." Tears rolled down my cheeks and for once I didn't bother trying to wipe them away. My heart felt like it was breaking and any questions I had regarding where things were going with Noah and I were quickly answered.

"Don't make any decisions tonight. You're upset, and you have every right to be. Take some time to let yourself think about how you feel and then talk to Noah. Just because he's having a baby with someone else doesn't mean that you can't be part of his life."

"I know. I just feel so betrayed by him. I asked him and he said no. Then I have to find out from some girl that I'll be working with 5 days a week? How am I supposed to be able to work with her and NOT think about them having sex?"

"I get it, I would feel the same way if some girl from Chase's past came back into our lives. But Jade, you forget that you are an AMAZING woman who is capable of so much. You're not a jealous, vindictive person. Once you take some time to process everything and talk to Noah, you're going to be just fine. She's not a threat to you honey."

Mia's words really hit and I was so thankful that she took the time to talk to me because it was just what I needed. She was right, I wasn't this person. I needed to think about how I felt about everything and sit down and talk with Noah. No one could decide our future except for us. There were plenty of families that were blended, beautiful messes, and if we had to- we could be one too.

"Thanks, Mia. You truly are the best. I appreciate you being there for me tonight."

"Of course. You sure you're going to be okay?"

"I'll be just fine, I promise."

"Alright. Well I better get going, Ry just woke up and she's hungry. It hasn't even been 24 hours since she was born and all this girl wants to do is eat." She giggled and I smiled, though part of me felt sad that I wouldn't be able to share this first with Noah. He would share all of the firsts regarding a new baby with a woman he doesn't even know.

"Go feed that sweet girl, and text me if you guys need anything." I smiled as I hung up and put my phone on the coffee table before laying back against the pillows and closing my eyes. There was a lot to think about and I needed a clear head before I even attempted talking to Noah. I heard my phone buzz on the table and ignored the new text message from him. He had been sending them all night but I gave up reading them for now. A few deep breaths and I could feel my body relaxing as I drifted off to sleep on the couch.

<u>Six</u>
Noah

I sighed as I sat my phone down on my desk and glared at the clock. It was 8:30 and Jade hadn't responded to a single text that I had sent. I felt so anxious after leaving the hospital that I decided to come into work in an effort to avoid showing up at her apartment and begging her to talk to me. I knew that she needed space but I found it increasingly harder to give it to her. I looked down and checked my phone again, the message still showing as delivered, not read.

It was close to closing time so I grabbed my phone and shoved it in my pocket as I went up front to help the new girl wrap things up for the night. I had hoped to have her better trained before Mia went on maternity leave but for whatever reason, we fell behind schedule which meant I was working a lot more hours than I usually did. And now with Chase taking a few weeks off to be home with Mia and the baby, I was going to be covering his side as well. Maybe the extra work would be good for me and keep me distracted until Jade was willing to talk.

I had been replaying the scene in the hospital over and over in my head all night. She was furious with me for not telling her and while I assumed she knew what happened with Cindy, I was too much of a coward to say anything to her about it. Never in my life had I ever regretted a one-night stand as much as I regretted that one. Jade and I had just broken up and I had been out drinking to blow off some steam. Cindy was a beautiful girl, thick and curvy with long brown hair that had wrapped nicely around my fist as she straddled me and told me all of the filthy things she wanted to do to me. I had to admit, I was pretty impressed with her dirty talk but even more impressed with her take-charge attitude, including when she surprised me with a blow job that ended with her rolling a condom on my dick before sliding me inside of her as she rode me.

A night of fun, while I was in a dark place, was now costing me something that meant more to me than anything else ever could. I knew I should have told Jade and it had been eating at me that I didn't have the balls to tell her this morning when she mentioned her. I knew who it was the second I heard the name. We didn't have anyone named Cindy in Haven Brook and what was the likelihood of someone with the same name showing up to work with Jade and being someone totally different? It was my luck that I would finally find someone to fall in love with only to have it ruined by a night of drunken stupidity.

I walked through the door that led from the back offices into the restaurant and made my way to the bar area off to the left. Julia was busy waiting on a few tables when I saw a woman sitting at the bar. I slid around the corner and grabbed a coaster from the back counter before turning around and placing it in front of the woman.

"Hey, what can I get you?" I asked as my eyes slowly made their way up from the countertop to the curvy brunette sitting in front of me. My heart stopped as I looked at Cindy who was smiling at me with a hint of mischief.

"Hey, stranger." She smiled as she folded her hands on top of each other on the bar top in front of her.

"Hey." My mind raced as I thought of what to say to her. The hardest part was that I didn't want to say anything to her. I felt furious with her as I looked at her, thinking about how if it wasn't for her, Jade would still be talking to me.

I took a deep breath and leaned back against the counter behind me, careful not to accidentally bump the handles on the beer tower behind me.

"It's been a while." Her eyes watched me cautiously.

"Yeah, it has been a while. You back in town for a quick visit?" While I already knew the answer since she was working with Jade, I wanted to hear from her what her actual plan was.

"I actually just moved here. So I'll be here for good." She smiled and looked down at her lap before looking back up at me.

"Well, I'm sure you'll like it here. It's not that different from Eastern Point." I pushed off the counter, ready to be done with the conversation. "Did Julia already take your order or was there something I could get you?"

"Just water is fine. I don't drink these days."

Something about the way her tone changed made my stomach drop. She scooted off of the barstool and stepped back, revealing a very round bump under the white sweater she was wearing with thick leggings. My eyes followed her hands as they ran over her stomach and cradled it.

"It looks like we have some talking to do." Her voice was quiet even though it sounded like it was screeching through my head. My eyes looked up at her, a mix of emotions on my face.

"We used a condom."

"Yeah, well, they aren't always effective. Obviously." She pointed at her stomach and smiled.

"Are you sure that it's mine?"

In an instant, the smile she had on her face quickly turned into a scowl as she stared at me like I had just asked the most ridiculous question she had ever heard.

"I'm not that kind of girl, so it DEEPLY bothers me that you would even ask that question." Her jaw was clenched tight as she gritted her teeth, each word filled with anger.

How the fuck was I supposed to know what kind of girl she was? I barely knew her for twenty minutes before she was using her mouth to roll a condom on me before fucking me senseless. She was a good lay, I would admit that, but it irritated me that she felt so entitled to something more given we didn't even know each other.

"I'm sorry, I didn't mean to offend you. But as you remember, we didn't know each other before that night and this is the first we've talked since then, so surely you can imagine how well I know you and how well you know me." My eyes drifted past her as Julia walked by, carrying a tray of empty glasses to the back as she cleared her last table. It was almost nine and time to close up.

I looked back at Cindy who stayed staring at me, waiting for me to say something. It felt like a trap and I had no clue what she was expecting. This wasn't the first time I had heard of a girl coming back, claiming she was pregnant from a one-night stand but I never thought I would be on the receiving end as the guy.

"So, what is your plan?" I asked, hoping to speed this process along.

"Well, I think we need to sit down and talk about stuff. This baby will be a part of your life and we need to figure out what that looks like."

"What do you mean what it looks like? Like joint custody after it's born?" My brows furrowed together.

I watched as her nostrils flared, the sweet girl I had met six months ago replaced by the angry pregnant woman in front of me.

"I was hoping that you would be the kind of guy who did the right thing from the start. Like go with me to my prenatal appointments and ultrasounds. Help me decorate the nursery. Pick out names together. You know, the stuff people usually do when they're having a baby."

"In all fairness- you're just now telling me about a baby that you've known about for six months. That makes it kind of hard to do the right thing. We can find some time later this week or this weekend to sit down and talk about living arrangements for the baby and you can give me the dates for your appointments and we will try to be there." I squared my shoulders and waited for her response.

"Who is we?" Her eyes pulled together as she glared at me.

"My girlfriend, Jade. She'll be a part of this as well." I had decided then and there that I wasn't about to let this ruin what I had with Jade. I prayed that Jade would let me talk to her and beg her for forgiveness for putting us in this predicament to begin with. Even if she didn't, I wanted Cindy to be fully aware that there was another woman in the picture and that this wasn't going to be her and I falling in love and starting a family together. We had one night of fun that resulted in a major responsibility which I was willing to accept, but that didn't mean that I had to end things with Jade.

She pursed her lips together and continued to glare at me.

"Well then, I guess WE will all talk soon. Here's my phone number and where I'll be staying if you come to your senses and decide you want to give this another shot. You know, be a good daddy for your child." She rolled her eyes as she turned on her heel and walked out the front door. I looked down at the paper she had handed me and debated whether or not to tear it up. It didn't matter either way. Nothing mattered until I talked to Jade and explained my side to her. I wrapped up closing and jumped in my truck, heading to Jade's apartment.

It was after 9:30 when I got there which felt like it took forever, yet it wasn't enough time for me to figure out what to say to her. She already knew that I had slept with someone else, that much was clear now from the conversation we had at the hospital. And given that she worked with Cindy, she also knew that she was pregnant. Jade wasn't stupid and I wasn't about to treat her like she was.

I made it up to her apartment rather quickly and knocked on the door, wondering if I should have called or text to let her know that I was coming over. Not that it would have mattered given that she hadn't read any of my other messages I had been sending all night. I took a deep breath before knocking again, debating on whether to leave or keep pushing my luck to try to get her to open the door and talk to me. A few seconds later I heard the locks click as the door slowly opened. I expected her to stand there and yell at me or slam the door in my face but surprisingly she moved to the side and nodded her head for me to come in.

"I thought for sure you were going to slam the door in my face," I admitted as I stepped inside and slipped out of my jacket before laying it on the back of the barstool behind me. Her apartment was bigger than most in the city and totally felt like Jade. Instead of a traditional dining room table, she had opted for a high-top table and barstools where we had spent a lot of time playing poker with Chase and Mia after she moved in. Her kitchen flowed into the living room, which always felt lively with the bright colors scattered around the room with rugs, pillows, and paintings along the wall. It fit who Jade was perfectly and my heart sank when I saw the puffiness around her eyes, knowing she had been crying. The room that usually felt bright and cheery now felt dark and gloomy.

"I'm not that immature, Noah." She sighed as she walked past me and curled up under a blanket on the sectional couch that took up the majority of the living room. I walked over and sat down beside her, desperate to talk things out with her and find the happiness we had this morning before everything had gone to hell.

"I know that you're not." I ran a hand through my hair and looked at her as if she would magically say the words to make everything better. As much as I knew this was my fault and I needed to be the one to make things right, I had no idea how to actually do that. The only thing that I knew how to do was flirt with women and lure them with my sexual abilities. I seriously doubted that it would work for me in this situation.

"I'm so sorry Jade. I screwed up and I'm sorry." I waited for her to answer as she looked over at me, the pissed off girl from the hospital making another appearance. I groaned and leaned back against the couch, pulling a bright yellow pillow into my side as I prayed that maybe it would force some happiness into the room.

"Noah, I'm trying very hard not to strangle you right now."

My eyebrow arched as I watched her pull her bottom lip in between her teeth and glare at me. On the surface, Jade looked pissed. But there was something in her eyes that went a little deeper, something that showed me how hurt she was. Not that I was happy that she was hurting, but I knew that if she was hurting then it meant that she still cared about me and that there was a way for me to save what we had. Going on a whim I decided to try a different approach and prayed that it wouldn't blow up in my face like everything else had today.

"Well, I'm not usually into that but we can give it a try. Erotic asphyxiation sounds a little kinky but I'm down for it if you are." I winked and waited to see what her reaction was. Her eyes gave her away as the green turned a shade darker before she got up and stormed into the kitchen. I had seen that look before and knew that she wasn't as mad at me as she was trying to let on.

I got up and followed her into the kitchen, standing directly behind her as she stood at the sink and filled a glass with water. I slowly kissed behind her ear, her hair pulled up into a messy bun on her head. I could feel her body responding to me as I kept alert to make sure the water wasn't thrown in my direction if she changed her mind.

"It's not going to work, Noah." She sighed as she turned around and pushed me away with one hand, taking a few steps away from me. I could see the frustration on her face as she warred over whether she wanted to stay mad at me or not.

"Are you sure about that?" I stepped closer, keeping my eyes on her as I closed the distance between us. She watched me as she tried to act like she wasn't feeling the electricity between us, stepping to the side before I could fully close the gap.

"Yeah, I'm sure," she snapped, crossing her arms over her chest before she tried to step past me again.

It was a bold move but honestly, I've done worse. I stepped directly in front of her, forcing her palms to hit my chest as she tried to avoid contact. I could see her pull her bottom lip in as her eyes darkened. Most guys would take it as a warning to back off and leave her alone, I took it as a challenge. I smiled coyly as my hands slowly reached forward and gently pushed her backward by her hips, her body resisting every step we took. Within a few short steps, her back was up against the kitchen counter, my arms pinning her in on both sides.

"So what? You want some sort of angry sex? You want me to tell you all the things that you do that piss me off while I fake an orgasm?" She jerked her head to the side, her eyes squinted in anger. Fuck. I knew she was mad but this was a side of her I hadn't seen before. And honestly, the more she spoke to me that way, the more my dick twitched. I might not be good at apologizing and begging for forgiveness, but I was good at worshipping her and showing her how much I fucking wanted her.

I took another step toward her, invading more of her space as she leaned her arms back against the counter to avoid touching me. Her words were telling me all of the reasons she was pissed at me while her body was screaming for me to give her the release she desperately wanted. Her shoulders were pulled back as her head looked away from me in annoyance, her pelvis slightly tilted toward me. I smiled as I moved closer, lining myself up so she could feel how hard I was through her thin yoga pants.

She let out a small gasp as her eyes darted toward me before looking away again.

"Since when have you ever faked an orgasm with me?" I whispered as I leaned close to her ear and softly kissed her neck. "Last I remember, you have at least 2-3 without me even trying." I leaned up and playfully nipped at her earlobe. I could feel her breathing change and knew that I was getting to her.

"But...." I leisurely ran my tongue down her neck and over her collarbone, feeling a faint shiver from her beneath me.

"If you want me to stop..." My tongue hovered right above the black lace of her bra that peeked up over her tank top, "just say the word."

Her body was still as my head lingered by her full breasts, the rise and fall starting to hypnotize me.

"Noah..," she warned as I bit the fabric and slowly tugged it down, exposing her nipple. I looked up at her under hooded eyes as she watched me, desire flushing across her face. I knew Jade well enough to know how her body reacted to me when she was turned on. When her hips softly rotated, allowing me direct access, I knew she wanted this more than she would ever admit.

"Just say the word, Jade." I pulled her nipple into my mouth, forcing her back to arch in response. I would be willing to bet that she was soaking wet for me already which made my dick feel like it was going to burst at any moment with all of the buildup. Her head fell back as she allowed me to work my tongue over her other nipple, both breasts on full display for my pleasure.

"Tell me, what do you want?" I ran a hand up and firmly grabbed her breast, flicking the nipple with my thumb as I planted kisses up the side of her neck. Her body swayed with mine, responding to every touch. I pushed into her again, showing her just how much I wanted to be inside her already as a soft moan escaped her throat.

"I'm still mad…" she whimpered with closed eyes as her hands wrapped around my neck and through my hair.

"Good," I growled, ready to get her naked and be inside of her already.

"Good?!" Her eyes shot open, anger on her face as she reached out to push me away.

"Yeah, because I'm about to fuck it out of you." I gave her the cockiest smile I had before leaning in and kissing her as my hands worked to get her shirt and bra off in record time. My eyes lowered to take in the sight of Jade before me, her beautiful body full of perfection. Her hands braced against me as I trailed kisses down her stomach before sinking to my knees and pulling her pants down, slowly taking her panties with them.

I looked up and watched her as I leaned forward and licked her slit. Her hand grabbed my hair as she bit her lip, watching as my tongue pushed in and out of her. I let out a chuckle as her hips started to grind against my face, her hand fully wrapped in my hair, pulling it harder the closer she got to climax.

"Spread for me, baby," I commanded as she slowly stepped to the side, spreading her legs. I ran a hand up her calf and grabbed her thigh, pulling it up over my shoulder immediately giving me more access as I pushed my face closer. I could feel her body responding as her breathing quickened and she pushed her hips down to get more pressure where she needed it. I smiled and groaned as I grabbed her other leg and pulled it over my shoulder so her pussy was right in my face as she leaned against the cabinet behind her. I flicked my tongue back and forth inside her, sucking up all of her wetness while focusing on her clit.

"Noah... Noah..." she panted heavily, my name never sounding more arousing than it did at that moment. I knew she was right there, ready for a release as I sucked harder, pushing her over the edge. Her body clenched as she dug her heels into my back, her body shaking in response against my tongue.

I waited until her body stopped quivering before helping her to her feet. She looked down at me as I slowly stood up and stood in front of her. I wanted to be inside of her, to forget everything that had happened today, and just make love to her. She watched the pained expressions on my face as she reached up and cupped my cheek, stroking it gently with her thumb. I closed my eyes and felt her pull me closer to her as she wrapped me in a hug and held me, everything I had weighing on me slowly slipping away.

"I am so sorry, Jade. I can't say it enough." I shook my head as the mood shifted and a darkness fell upon us.

"I know you are," she whispered, still holding my face.

"I should have told you. I never should have even slept with her, but I was drunk and upset, and there's no excuse. I messed up. I fucked everything up."

I pulled back and ran a hand down my face as I turned away from her. She didn't deserve any of this. She deserved so much more than what I was giving her. I heard rustling behind me and knew that she was getting dressed. While I enjoyed going down on her and giving her the release she needed, I knew that it didn't solve any of the problems that were still surrounding us.

"You did fuck up, Noah. But only with not telling me. We weren't together when you slept with her and I knew that. I'm not mad at you for sleeping with her- don't get me wrong- I'm not happy about it either. But I can't hold it against you for sleeping with her when we were broken up. We hadn't been together that long before we broke up so I get it. I knew who you were before we started dating, that's why I asked you if you had been with anyone while we were apart." She looked into my eyes and I was relieved that she was willing to have an honest, mature discussion about this.

As hard as it was to talk about, I was thankful that we didn't have to have a ton of drama. I would spend the rest of my life making this up to Jade if she would let me, I had no problem admitting that I had made a huge mistake that hurt her tremendously.

"I was really hurt when we broke up. I didn't know how to deal with it and next thing I knew, I was going back to old habits." I shrugged as we made our way over to the couch and sat down.

"I know." She gave a half-smile as she nodded in agreement.

"I never meant to hurt you, Jade. I swear. When you said her name this morning, I couldn't believe that it was the same person. I was stressed all day trying to figure out what to do. I wanted to tell you because you deserved to know, but at the same time, as cowardly as it sounds, I didn't want to tell you because I wanted to protect you from the pain that I ended up causing with all of this." I watched as a tear slid down her face, my hand desperate to reach over and wipe it away for her.

"I was pretty blindsided when I sat across from a very pregnant woman who was going on and on about how she moved here to be with the man she loves and is having a baby with. When she described him as gorgeous with black hair and hazel eyes, I knew it was you."

"I'm so sorry that you had to find out that way. She showed up at The Vine tonight and I'll admit, I was pretty fucking surprised to see that she's pregnant."

"She showed up at your work?" Jade's eyes narrowed.

"Yeah, right before closing."

"Did she know you worked there from when you guys got together before?"

"No, we didn't bother talking about anything personal. I was out drinking with Wyatt and we were at Malarkey's when I met her."

"How did she know you would be there?"

"I have no idea. It's a small-town thing, people know everything about you whether you want them to or not. All she had to do was ask around a few places and someone would point her to The Vine."

"That's true, I guess." She sighed as she leaned into the cushion and stretched her legs across the couch. I reached over and lifted them up as I scooted over and rubbed them for her.

"So, what does all of this mean? I mean, you're having a baby with a woman you don't even know." Her eyes searched mine, looking for an answer to a question she hadn't asked.

"I don't know, honestly. She wants me to be there for all of her appointments and to help set up the nursery and stuff. I've never been in this situation before so I'm not sure what I'm supposed to do. Chase shot daggers at me earlier when I asked if he should be at home helping Mia practice her breathing before she went into labor, so obviously, I have no fucking clue what to do with pregnant women." I smiled as Jade laughed and for a moment, everything between us felt like it was going to be alright.

"Did you tell her about me?"

"I did, I told her that we would find time soon where we could all sit down together and figure everything out. I mean it, Jade, just because I'm having an unexpected baby with another woman, that doesn't mean that I want anything between us to change. And honestly, I really meant it earlier when I said that I thought you should move in with me."

My hands started sweating as I realized what I had said before I took a moment to think about it. At the hospital, I didn't know if I actually wanted Jade to move in with me or if I was just saying it because I was feeling desperate. Now that it came out of me so naturally, I felt like maybe I was ready for the next step in our relationship. Jade studied me nervously as she thought about my proposal to live together. I knew that I had lost her trust but I was willing to do whatever it took to earn it back.

"Are you sure that we're ready for that?" There was a hesitation in her voice that killed me and I hated that she had to doubt everything about our relationship because I made a terrible mistake and kept it from her for six months.

"I'm ready for it. Are you?"

She let out a deep breath as she looked around the apartment. I braced myself for her to say no. I couldn't blame her.

"Can we just keep doing what we're doing? Where I stay at your place sometimes, and you stay at mine? I'm not ready to give up my apartment just yet, it's the only thing I have that is really me. I love this apartment and IF something were to happen, I wouldn't want to be stuck trying to find something else."

"Fair enough." I smiled, trying to hide the disappointment I felt that she wasn't ready to give up her life so freely like I had wanted. When I thought about it, that was exactly what I was asking her to do. Give up everything she had worked for her since she came here on her own, and come live with me in my house. If the question was reversed, would I be willing to walk away from everything I had worked so hard to build for myself? My stomach hardened as the answer stared me in the face.

"I'm sorry Noah, I know you're disappointed. I just don't want us to do something out of impulse because there's suddenly other changes around us." Her voice was soft as she ran a hand up and cupped my cheek.

"It's okay," I whispered as I pulled her across the couch and wrapped my arms around her.

<u>Seven</u>
Jade

Yesterday felt like a whirlwind of a day, between training a new girl at work who just happened to be carrying my boyfriend's baby, to Mia having her baby, to Noah and I working things out. There was a lot packed into a very small window which explained why I woke up this morning feeling like a truck ran me over a few times.

I worked on getting my hair pulled up into a sleek ponytail before applying another coat of mascara to my overly tired-looking eyes. Growing up my mom could always tell the days that I truly didn't feel well because my eyes would change from a dark green to a grayish color, and today they were definitely gray. I quickly applied some red lipstick and gave myself one more glance before grabbing my purse and heading off to work.

Noah and I had spent a few hours last night talking through everything which seemed to help my overall mindset about what had happened. There was so much going through my mind before he got there that once I saw him at the door, I was almost relieved to just deal with everything right then and there so we could get it over with.

I wanted to be mad at Noah. Furious at him. But every time I thought about it in my head I kept reminding myself that the only thing he actually did wrong was lie to me about whether he had slept with anyone while we were broken up. I had already accepted that I had no right to be mad at him for the things he did when we were broken up, especially when I was the one who had decided to break up with him. Neither of us knew at the time whether we would get back together, our lifestyles too restless for each other. We weren't the type of people who wanted to settle down and I was already feeling the itch to go somewhere and do something different.

People have always said that I'm such a free spirit, that I have it in my blood to wander and roam without wanting to be tied down. The truth is that I grew up with a single mom who moved us every time she would start to get close to someone. If there was the opportunity for a real relationship to develop, we were out of there before the thought could even process in their mind. She would always say that it's always best to leave before you get attached. You can't get hurt if you don't stick around to let them. Leave them before they can leave you.

Those were the things that I grew up learning and to this day I've yet to have an adult relationship where I've stayed long enough for it to turn into something. Until now. Now I have Noah and for the first time in my life, I don't want to run. I don't want to get out before it's too late. Until yesterday I was playing around with the idea of what our future might look like someday.

I pulled into the parking lot of the bank and glanced into the rearview mirror, giving myself a quick mini pep talk before I had to walk in those doors and see the woman who had caused so much havoc in such a short period of time. I opened the door and grabbed my purse and cellphone from the middle console, seeing a text message from Noah. I smiled as I opened it.

Noah: Good morning, beautiful. Have a wonderful day and don't forget to send me some nudes on your break.

I laughed as I rolled my eyes and sent back a quick good morning message before tossing my phone back into my purse. I pulled my shoulders back and walked into the building with the confidence of a woman who didn't just find out that her boyfriend was having a baby with her coworker.

Relief settled over me as I made my way to my desk and noticed that Cindy wasn't there yet. I opened the bottom drawer and sat my purse inside, tossing my keys on top. This morning had been such a rush that I hadn't given myself time to make coffee and I instantly regretted it. I wandered off to the break room after closing the drawer, making sure my purse was secure. There weren't a ton of coffee drinkers here that didn't bring their own coffee from home so the likelihood that someone would have made a pot of coffee was slim. I walked into the break room disappointed when the coffee pot sat in its usual spot, empty. I sighed and decided to give up on the idea, my motivation for anything pretty lacking at the moment.

As I started heading toward my desk I noticed someone bent over, leaning toward the bottom drawer where my purse was. I tried to walk as quietly as I could, keeping my heels from clicking too hard on the tile floor. As I got closer I noticed the brown hair before Cindy popped up, startled. My eyes narrowed together as I crossed my arms over my chest and glared at her, waiting for an answer.

"Hi!" Her face flushed red as she tried to sit upright as quickly as possible as she tried to shut the drawer with her foot. I tilted my head to the side, one eyebrow arched, as I watched her do it. Her face turned a darker color of red as she stood up and moved away from my desk, coming around to the other side where she is supposed to sit.

"Is there a reason that you're going through my personal things?" I walked past her and stood on the other side of the desk, placing my palms flat on the desk as I leaned forward and waited for her to answer. She shifted uncomfortably in her seat before looking up at me and making eye contact.

"I'm sorry, I was looking for a notepad so I could take notes." She looked away and I knew she was lying. Hell, I knew she was lying the moment I caught her red-handed.

"Like that one?" I nodded to the notepad and pen that were sitting neatly on the desk in front of her that I had purposely sat out the night before.

"Oops. Guess I should have looked here first."

I let out a deep breath as I tried to focus on being professional and not reaching forward to rip her head off like I really wanted to.

"Look, Cindy, we need to have some boundaries and those will include you respecting my personal space. If you need something, you need to ask before you go helping yourself." I stared at her as she nodded slightly before looking away.

I sat down and leaned over to look inside the drawer to see what she could have been messing with. My purse looked exactly the same as how I had left it and nothing else looked like it had been moved. My desk was always clean and organized which meant she didn't have a lot of time to snoop around in the few minutes I was gone. I closed the drawer and opened the one above it, pulling out the training material that we hadn't finished the day before. As my irritation with her increased so did my regret for not making coffee.

It was almost nine which meant the lobby would be opening soon. I could try to run quickly to the back to make a pot of coffee or I could wait it out and see if any of the customers asked for coffee, which would mean someone would end up making a pot. It was a gamble since we weren't usually busy on Tuesdays but I didn't trust Cindy by herself at my desk so I had no choice but to skip it.

I spent a few minutes sorting through the training materials on my desk while having Cindy review her notes from yesterday in an effort to stall until I could get my head straight and work with her. The door chimed up front and out of the corner of my eye I watched as the receptionist walked back to her desk as someone followed behind her.

I expected the person to head to the teller line or sit in the waiting area for a loan officer, instead a pair of steel-toed boots stood beside my desk. As I slowly looked up, the smell of coffee floated around me.

"Hey, beautiful. Thought you might need this today." Noah sat the to-go cup of coffee on my desk and sat on the corner of it, out of the way from the pile I had created. Behind him, I saw Cindy's eyes go wide with the shock of seeing him at my desk and I wondered if she knew I was the girlfriend he had told her about. I smiled as I stood up and wrapped my arms around his neck, hugging him a little too tight for it to be appropriate in the workplace.

"Thanks, baby. You have no idea how badly I need this today." I pulled back and smiled, genuinely happy to see him while not giving a damn that Cindy was now glaring at our interaction.

"No problem. Anything to keep my girl happy." He reached forward and gently pinched my chin between his fingers before slightly looking over his shoulder to acknowledge Cindy.

"Morning."

"Good morning," she replied tightly before shifting her attention back to her notes.

"Well, I better get going. I have a lot to do with Chase being out this week on his little vacation." He rolled his eyes as I playfully swatted his shoulder.

"He's not on vacation, he's being a good husband and helping Mia with their beautiful new baby." I smiled warmly at him before second-guessing talking about babies with the situation sitting in front of me. While I didn't want to keep Noah from being involved in his child's life, I also didn't want Cindy overstepping into ours. And given I was already irritated with her for going through my personal stuff, this made everything feel even more awkward.

"Either way." He chuckled and stood up, planting a kiss on my forehead. "See you tonight?"

"Sounds good," I whispered, wanting to keep our relationship a little more private with Cindy so close.

"Bye, Cindy," He called out over his shoulder and walked out the door.

I sat down at my desk and pulled myself closer, reaching for the coffee and taking a sip. Within seconds I could feel the heat flowing through my body, calming me in the process.

"Alright, let's get started." I grabbed the pile that we needed to get through as Cindy's head whipped up, a pissed off look on her face.

"You two seem happy, have you been together long?"

The way she asked the question had my blood boiling.

"Noah and I are very happy, and I'm sorry, but my personal business is none of yours." I looked at her as I picked up my coffee cup and took another sip. I may not have had a lot of romantic relationships in my life but I've had plenty of times where I've had to stand up for myself which made dealing with Cindy easy.

"Well then I'm sure he's told you about our situation and how we will all be involved, so I guess that does make your personal life my business."

"How so?" I leaned forward resting my forearms on my desk while straightening my posture.

"Because Noah will want to be in his child's life and that means that as the mother, I get a say in who is in his. I may not want someone toxic around my child." She jutted her jaw forward and rubbed a hand over her stomach.

"Look, there are a lot of things that the three of us will need to discuss soon. However, this is not the time or the place to do so. If you're unable to keep your personal life separate then maybe you should look at another job that allows you to do so." I took a deep breath and leaned back against my chair. "I will not continue to train you if this is going to continue to be an issue."

I watched as the color drained from her face and she lowered her hands to her lap.

"I really need this job."

"Then I suggest we make an effort to work together."

She nodded her head yes in agreement as I took another long drink of coffee, thankful to have a little ammunition on my side today.

<u>Eight</u>
Noah

I leaned down and checked on the food in the oven before opening a bottle of wine as I waited for Jade to get here. Last night was a long night and even after I left her apartment feeling better that we had talked things out, I still felt like I needed to prove my love to her in so many ways. Especially since I was completely head over heels in love with her and we hadn't actually said it to each other yet.

I had skipped out of work an hour early after our regular temp, Stacy, offered to pick up some hours with Chase and Mia being out of the office. I loved Stacy and she had worked with us for so long that I trusted her to run the place as much as I trusted Chase. She would watch over Julia tonight which left me confident that the two of them would be just fine without me. And the worst-case scenario, I was just a phone call away if not.

It was almost 5:30 and Jade should be there any second. I poured the glasses of wine and sat them on the table that had already been set with candles and a basket of bread in between the plates and salad bowls. I pulled the chicken parmigiana out of the oven right when the doorbell rang and called for her to come in over my shoulder while I dealt with the hot pan. I sat it on top of the stove, sliding the oven mitts off when I turned to go open the door since I hadn't heard the familiar sound of Jade's heels across the floor as she came in.

As I spun around I was stopped in my tracks by Cindy standing in front of me.

"Cindy? What are you doing here?" My brows pulled together as I watched her look past me to the table I had worked hard on setting up for my romantic dinner with Jade.

"You said to come in."

"I thought it was Jade. What are you doing here?" I crossed my arms over my chest and watched her as her eyes filled with tears.

"I'm sorry. I should go." She turned to leave. Part of me wanted to let her but the other part wasn't a complete dick.

"Why are you here?" My tone was softer as I leaned against the counter behind me, watching the door for Jade.

"I didn't know where else to go, I don't know anyone in town. I just needed a friend." Her voice was low as she looked down at the ground and played with the drawstring on her coat.

"Okay, so what's going on?" I was starting to lose my patience the longer she moped in my kitchen, knowing that it would ruin the ambiance I had worked so hard to create for Jade if she walked in and saw her here.

"I don't think Jade likes me and I thought maybe we could talk about it?"

I blew out a frustrated breath as I pushed off from the counter and looked at her.

"Look, I'm more than happy to talk to you about this later. Right now isn't a good time."

"You're right, I shouldn't have just come over unannounced." She let out a heavy sigh as she turned to leave, almost running into Jade on her way out the door. I watched as Jade's face changed the moment she saw Cindy, the anger flickering in her eyes as she looked between the two of us.

"We'll talk later, thanks again." She smiled warmly as she walked past Jade as she stepped inside, leaving plenty of room for Cindy to leave. The door closed leaving an awkward silence behind. Jade glared at the door before turning her attention to me.

"Jade, I'm so sorry-"

"Don't." She put her hand up to stop me.

"But-"

"Noah, did you do all of this?" She gestured to the romantic dinner beside me.

"Yes." I swallowed hard, praying that all of this wasn't ruined after all. I watched as Jade sat her purse on the coffee table and kicked her heels off before she came running over to me, wrapping her legs around my waist and pulling me in for a kiss. I wrapped my arms around her as our lips stayed pressed against each other, feeling the comfort from her body as she wrapped it around mine.

"You surprise me, Mr. Wilder." She leaned forward and kissed me again before unwrapping her legs and sliding down to the floor. Her ponytail swayed from side to side as she shook her head back and forth in amazement as she walked around the table and took in the details.

"Oh yeah?"

"Yup. I would have never imagined you to be a candlelight dinner kind of guy." She smiled up at me as she stood behind the chair, her eyes filled with happiness. My heart started to go back to normal as I allowed myself to relax with her, fear of the evening being ruined by Cindy dissipating.

"I'll be whatever kind of guy you want me to be." I ran a hand across her lower back where her silk blouse was tucked into her black dress slacks.

"I just want you to be you." Her eyes searched mine as she reached a hand up and gently stroked my cheek. I raised my hand to hold hers before placing a kiss on it.

"Have a seat and I'll get dinner served before it gets cold." I pulled out her chair and waited until she was seated before I scooted behind her to grab the pan of chicken. Thankfully, everything was still hot and fresh, just like my mom assured me it would be. I had heard the change in her tone when I had told her what I was trying to do. She contained her excitement the best she could before squealing for me to call her tomorrow to let her know how everything went.

I sat the plates on the table in front of us with a generous serving of chicken parmigiana and noodles accompanied by steamed asparagus.

Jade's eyes went wide and she tried to hide her surprise when she realized that I had actually cooked and not ordered takeout. I ignored the giant pile of dirty dishes in the sink as I grabbed the salad from the fridge and brought it to the table.

"Noah, everything looks and smells delicious. This is amazing!"

"I'm happy you like it. Now let's just hope it tastes as good as it looks," I joked as I sat the rest of the salad down on the counter behind me and joined Jade at the table.

We ate in silence as we enjoyed the wine and every now and then I would hear her moan as she took a bite that she enjoyed. I tried to keep myself distracted and focused on eating instead of thinking about how hot she sounded as she enjoyed the meal. If I would have known that she could sound that fucking sexy while eating, I would have started cooking for her a long time ago. It would give a whole different meaning to appetizers and four-course meals.

"Oh my gosh, I am so stuffed. This was one of the best meals I've ever had." She leaned back against the chair and smiled at me as she lazily brought the glass of wine to her lips and took a sip. I licked my lips, jealous of the glass she was holding, and adjusted my jeans to give me some relief from the tightness she was creating.

"I'm glad you enjoyed it." I mimicked her and leaned back against the seat as I finished the wine in my glass.

"There's a lot that I enjoy with you."

"Same here." My eyes darkened as I thought about how much I wanted to enjoy her. Right here.
Right now.

"You cooked so, I'll clean up." She scooted her chair back and stood up, grabbing her plate and salad bowl from the table.

"I don't think so." I stepped beside her and grabbed them from her, sitting them on the counter. "The dishes can wait, I'll do them later."

"Noah, that's silly. I can help clean up," she protested as she put a hand on her hip and looked at me. Her eyes were back to dark green and not the gray they were when I saw her this morning. I loved that she was back to her sassy, sexy little self.

"I know you can, but tonight is about me showing you how much you mean to me." I slid an arm around her waist and pulled her into me, smelling the coconut smell of her shampoo.

"You don't have to do all of this, you know that right?" She pushed back and looked at me like I was crazy for wanting to show my love to her.

"I know that I don't have to. I want to." I looked down and studied her face as confusion settled in.

"Hasn't anyone ever done something like this for you before? Shown you how much they care about you?"

"No," she whispered before she looked away.

"Jade, you deserve to have someone show you how much they love you every single day."

Her eyes whipped up to look at me, panic on her face. Now was the moment that we both had been cautiously avoiding. The moment where the way we felt about each other would be more than just trying to show each other. It would be saying the words that we purposely avoided at all costs. The words that you couldn't take back once you said them.

"I love you, Jade."

Nine
Jade

I was by far the worst person in the world. Who lets their boyfriend make a romantic candlelight dinner and says I love you for the first time, and not say it back? The evening had progressed into a calm, relaxing night as we cuddled on the couch but I couldn't help but wonder what Noah thought when he told me he loved me and I didn't say it back.

Did I want to say it? Absolutely. One hundred percent. But something deep down wouldn't let me. Was it the fear my mom instilled in my sister and I from the time we were little to never let ourselves fall in love so easily? Or was it the result of watching my sister die at the hands of an abusive man that promised to love her and yet beat her every day from the time they said I do.

Maybe it wasn't any of that. Maybe it was that I walked in on Cindy inside Noah's house unexpectedly when I got here. Everything about Cindy felt like a trigger for me. No matter how hard I tried, I just didn't like her and didn't trust her. I could feel my shoulders getting tense from the thought of her, Noah's body responding to it right away.

"Everything okay?" He leaned to the side and looked at me as I stayed tucked into his side under his shoulder.

"Yeah, I'm fine." I gently rolled my shoulders a few times hoping it would help alleviate the tension.

"Do you want to talk about it?" His voice was soft in my ear as he held onto me, my body starting to relax into his. I let out a sigh as I debated whether I wanted to talk about it or not. Either way, I knew that we needed to if we wanted things to keep moving forward in our relationship. Now wasn't the time to have blocked communication or to keep things from each other.

"Why was Cindy here earlier?" I kept my gaze on the tv for fear of looking like a totally insecure and jealous girlfriend.

"Honestly, I don't know. I sure as hell wasn't expecting her. I thought it was you when she knocked and I told her to come in."

"What did she say?"

"Nothing really, just that she needed a friend to talk to." His voice trailed off and I knew there was more.

"Talk about what?" I turned slightly and looked up at him.

"She thinks that you don't like her."

"I don't." My answer was cold and blunt but there wasn't a need to try to sugarcoat it. I felt his chest move as he tried to stifle his laughter at my bluntness.

"I know that it sounds immature and petty but I don't like her. And not just because you slept with her and she got pregnant, I just don't trust her."

"Why not?" His eyes searched mine with genuine curiosity, making me feel comfortable having this discussion with him.

"This morning after I got to work I stepped away from my desk for a few minutes and when I came back I caught her sitting at my desk, going through my bottom drawer where I keep my purse."

His eyes got dark, his jaw clenching in response.

"Did you ask her about it?"

"Absolutely. She insisted that she was looking for a notepad to take notes with, then I pointed out there was one on the desk where she sits."

He nodded his head as he looked off across the room toward the door.

"I was very direct with her and told her we needed to have boundaries, that she wasn't to go through my stuff."

"Good. I'm sure that will help. Maybe it was just a misunderstanding?" I could hear the faint sound of hope in his voice that this wasn't as big of an issue as I was making it into.

"That's not all." I scooted away from him and turned to face him. I needed his full attention before I told him the rest.

"Okay.... what else happened?"

"After you left, she made a snide comment about how happy we seemed and asked how long we've been together." I blew out a deep breath before continuing. "I explained to her that we are happy but that my personal business is none of hers. She got REALLY defensive about how she's having a baby with you so that makes my business her business because she may not want toxic people in her baby's life."

I watched as Noah leaned back against the couch and pinched the bridge of his nose as he closed his eyes. His chest rose and fell heavily as he let out a sigh.

"I'm so sorry that you're getting caught up in all of this, Jade." His eyes met mine, sadness to them that wasn't there before.

"It's fine, I'm a big girl. I can handle myself."

"So what happened after that?"

"I explained to her that it was a place of business and that if she couldn't keep her personal business separate then maybe she needed to find a new place to work. Her attitude seemed to change after that and she told me she couldn't afford to lose this job. The rest of the day she was quiet and ended up leaving an hour early because she said she wasn't feeling well."

"Well, I can see why she would think you don't like her." His eyes lit up as he tried to hold his laughter inside. Playfully I reached over and swatted his chest.

"Oh stop it, I'm not that mean!" I tried to keep a straight face before my laughter mixed in with his as he pulled me over to him, tickling me until I was straddling his thighs.

"You are, in fact, very mean." He eyed me suspiciously, his hands maintaining a firm grip on my hips so I couldn't try to get away.

"Am I?" I licked my lips as I slowly lowered myself further down on top of him and ran my tongue up the side of his neck before playfully nibbling on his earlobe. I could feel the stretch of his jeans underneath me as I slowly rocked back and forth, his body reacting to every movement.

"I don't know that you wanna start something you can't finish." His voice was gruff in my ear as his hands helped guide my hips into the fluid motion as I continued to grind against him.

"Who said anything about not finishing?" Slowly I reached down and unbuttoned my silk blouse, taking my time with each button while my hips continued grinding lower against him. I could feel his erection bulging beneath, growing bigger by the second.

His eyes watched my every movement as I tossed the shirt to the side and reached back to unclasp my bra. I chewed my lip as I took my time sliding the bra strap down each arm, carefully holding the bra in place against my breasts. Without warning his hands flew up and grabbed the bra, throwing it to the side and freeing my breasts that were inches away from his face. I giggled as he swatted my hands away and ran his up my stomach and under each breast before slowly leaning forward and running his tongue over my nipple.

I leaned back, resting my hands on his thighs as he continued sucking my nipples and caressing my breasts. I could feel the pressure starting to build up, the need to feel him inside me growing stronger with each lick. I leaned forward and wrapped my arms behind his neck, pulling his hair as I tried to find a release. I needed out of these dress slacks and for him to be inside of me already.

I took a jagged breath and slowly pushed off, his eyes wild as they watched my every move. I stood in between his legs as I slowly unbuttoned the top button of my dress slacks, my hand firm on the zipper as I pulled it out down. As I was about to slide them down my legs I saw a reflection in the mirror of someone watching through the sliding glass door behind us.

I gasped as I quickly turned around, one hand covering my breasts while the other grabbed my pants to keep them up.

"What's wrong?" Noah jumped up beside me, his eyes quickly searching the room.

"Someone was outside watching us! I saw their reflection in the mirror, they were at the back door." I pointed to where I had seen them then quickly grabbed my pants before they fell down again.

Noah took off running past me and flung open the front door while I quickly grabbed my clothes off the couch and got dressed. A few minutes later Noah came back inside, out of breath as he closed the front door and locked it.

"Did you see anyone?"

"No, but a car took off as soon as I went outside. I tried to run after it but I didn't get a good look. It was a small car, a sedan of some sort. Red. That's all I got." He walked over and checked the sliding glass door before closing the blinds and coming over to the couch.

"A red car?" My stomach sank when everything started to click.

"Yeah, that's what it looked like. Why?"

"Cindy drives a red car."

<u>Ten</u>
Noah

I looked out into the open field, the sun starting to set behind the mountain casting a warm glow. I took a deep breath as I forced all of the worries and doubt out of me as I exhaled. People were starting to arrive and my hands were sweating as I looked back and saw the rows of white folding chairs creating an aisle that Jade would soon be walking down.

In the crowd I spotted my mom and dad, making their way toward the front row. Off in the distance, Chase was playing a quick game of catch with Liam and Grant, all of them dressed in black tuxedoes. The music started floating overhead as the pastor made his way up to the altar and stood next to me. Soon everyone had taken their seat and at the end of the walkway, I could see the wedding party lining up.

Chase and Mia were first in line as they pushed the stroller with Rylee in it, too little to actually throw rose petals, but still the most beautiful flower girl I had ever seen. Liam walked quickly down the aisle, holding onto the side of the stroller as he ignored the whispers from everyone around him on how handsome he looked.

Soon the wedding party had all made their way down the aisle and fanned out next to me as we turned our focus to Jade. The music changed and I listened carefully for the song she chose to come on. There was nothing. Just silence. I leaned forward and tried to see past the rows of chairs, looking for her.

Slowly she stepped forward, her face as beautiful as ever with her hair pinned perfectly upon her head. Her dress was stunning and showed off her curvy body including a pregnant belly. I swallowed hard as I looked beside her and saw Cindy. Suddenly music played overhead but it wasn't Jade's song. It was dark and ominous as it slowly got louder. I could see panic on Jade's face as she looked for me, reaching out her hand for me to come get her. I started to run toward her as everyone got up from their seats and started walking toward me, getting in the way.

My parents reached me first, my mom desperately clutching at her throat to try to stop the bleeding while my dad gasped for air, blood soaking his shirt. My eyes were wide with horror when I saw the knife wounds. Panic filled me as everyone around me started to drop dead on the floor, Chase and Mia cuddled together as she tried to rock Rylee whose face was covered in Mia's blood. No one was safe. Liam. Grant. Jade.

I watched in horror as Cindy smiled at me, a sharp knife in her hand as she grabbed Jade and drug her backward. I ran as fast as I could, darting in between chairs and dead bodies, desperate to get to Jade. The harder I ran, the bigger the distance was that separated us until there was nothing around me but dead loved ones as Jade disappeared with Cindy.

I felt ice-cold fingertips run across my chest as my eyes flew open, forcefully pushing them away. Jade jolted up, startled, as her eyes watched me with horror.

"I'm sorry..." I said as quickly as I realized that it was Jade that was touching me and that I had been having another nightmare.

"Are you okay?" She continued to watch me as she kept her distance on the other side of the bed.

"Yeah. I was having a bad dream, I didn't mean to scare you." I blew out a breath and sat up, leaning back against the headboard.

"It's okay, I could hear you panicking in your sleep. I was trying to wake you."

"Thank you." I reached over and gently patted her hand.

"I know that you don't ever want to talk about them, but I really think that you should. This is the 5th or 6th one that you've had while I've stayed over in the past two months. Something is obviously bothering you, Noah." Her eyes pleaded with mine. I patted the empty space on the bed next to me, relieved when she slid over and cuddled up against me.

"I've been having nightmares." I paused as I quickly debated whether I should even be telling her this. "About you."

I waited for her response, worried that she would take it the wrong way. Was there a right way?

"Okay. What happens in the dreams?"

I blew out another breath and ran a hand down my face.

"Terrible, horrible things." I closed my eyes and leaned my head back against the headboard.

"Noah...." I could hear the warning in her voice and had to laugh that she could be so bossy with getting me to tell her when most girls would be upset to find out that they were the source of my nightmares.

"It's different things. Someone takes you and I can't see who it is. They threaten to kill you. They've tried to kill you. They kill my family. They burn down my house while you're in it. Everything always leads back to them hurting or killing you and I can't do anything about it. This one was worse though."

"What happened in this one?"

I shook my head and looked away.

"Noah, what happened in this one?" She turned sideways and took my head in her hands, forcing me to look at her. "Tell me what happened."

"We were getting married. Everything was beautiful. White chairs spread out across the green field, the mountains in the distance with the sun setting. Everyone was there, my family, our friends. Everyone had walked down the aisle and I was waiting for you. But you never came. Then the music changed and you were in the back being held hostage by Cindy. And everyone around me was dying. My mom's throat was slit. My dad was stabbed. Chase. Mia. Rylee. No one was spared. I was trying to get to you but every step I took I only got farther away as Cindy smiled and pulled you further away from me as she held the knife that killed everyone."

Her eyes were soft as she pulled me towards her and wrapped her arms around me. She held me tightly as she kissed my face, planting kisses all over before landing on my lips. I could feel the weight of my dream lift off me the longer she held me, calmness settling over us. She pulled back and held my head in her hands, smiling at me.

"Thank you for telling me." She sighed but never let go, even as a quick flash of sadness crossed her face.

"Those are terrible dreams and I'm so sorry that you keep having them. I'm even more sorry that they're about me." She laughed and I felt the pull of a smile across my face. "But they are just dreams Noah, no one is ever going to take me away from you. Ever. Okay?"

I nodded yes as she wrapped herself around me again and at that moment I knew that I never wanted to be with anyone else.

"I should have said it earlier and I'm sorry that I didn't, but I love you too, Noah. I love you more than you could ever know."

I wrapped her in my arms and pulled her as close as I could, wanting to feel every tiny bit of love that we were sharing at that moment. If I could, I would have bottled it up so I wouldn't have to worry about ever losing it. If only I would've known...

Eleven
Jade

"How has it already been two weeks? I could swear you just had Rylee yesterday." I leaned closer to the bundle of blankets and took a deep breath, filling my lungs with the sweet smell of baby.

"I know, it's crazy! I was just telling Chase that we needed to have you and Noah over soon to catch up. Things have been so busy with the baby that I haven't been able to see straight and I know he's been looking forward to getting back to work. It would be nice to have a distraction too." Mia sighed as she leaned back against the couch and watched as I rocked Rylee back to sleep.

"It would be great to hang out with you guys, I miss seeing you all the time."

"I miss seeing you too."

"Should I put her down or is she okay to sleep on my shoulder?"

"She's fine where she's at unless you'd rather put her down. In that case, we can put her in her crib in the nursery."

I wrinkled my nose and frowned as I slowly sat down on the opposite end of the couch from Mia and sunk into the pillow while Rylee stayed sleeping on me. Mia let out a soft laugh, the lines under her eyes creasing in response.

She looked gorgeous for being a new mom who wasn't getting any sleep and I prayed that someday I would be able to look as good as she did. Her naturally blonde hair had been cut into a short bob that framed her face perfectly with side-swept bangs that made her baby blue eyes stand out. She was already beautiful but I thought motherhood had changed her for the better. There was a new softness that hadn't been there before.

"So, tell me what's new. Chase said that Noah is going with Cindy to her next ultrasound on Monday- how's everything going with that?"

"It's fine, I guess." I shrugged and debated how much of the Cindy drama I wanted to get into.

"Just fine?"

"He's putting a lot of effort into trying to be there for her and it feels like she's taking advantage of the situation."

"How so?" Mia's voice was gentle and lacked the judgmental tone I had gotten used to hearing from Cindy for the last few weeks.

"She uses the baby against him for everything. It's like she knows that he wants to do the right thing and be in the baby's life so she constantly threatens to take that away. He's been late to work a few times to show up at appointments that she doesn't tell him about until the last minute then claims that he didn't want to go or he would have been there on time. It's just hard watching him jump through hoops for her."

"Wow. I heard she was a little crazy but I didn't know that it was that bad." Mia smiled sympathetically as she leaned her head against the couch.

"Yeah, crazy might be an understatement." I shifted on the couch and gently patted the baby's back to keep her asleep. "Mia, are you sure you don't want to go lay down? I'm off the rest of the afternoon and don't mind watching Rylee so you can get some sleep while Chase is at work."

She looked exhausted and I suddenly felt bad for asking to come by last minute after I was told to take a half-day for the extra hours I had worked last week with getting Cindy trained and on a teller drawer. I didn't think twice before accepting their offer. I was out the door and on the phone with Mia before I even opened my car door.

"No, I'm okay. I'm always tired but I never get to visit with anyone. Trust me, I need this." She smiled as she tried to fight a yawn. Guilt flooded me as I realized how bad of a friend I had been for not checking in on her sooner. I had intended to give them time to get settled in with the new baby before coming by but the sadness on Mia's face when she said she doesn't get to visit with anyone made me regret not coming by sooner.

"If you're sure..." I eyed her carefully, waiting to see if she would change her mind.

"Yes, I'm sure." She playfully swatted at my leg and smiled.

"So how's Chase doing with all of the baby stuff?"

"Good, he's just as exhausted as I am. But he's been great at helping me with everything. He gets up with us in the middle of the night and handles the diaper changes since I'm the only one that can feed her. Granted we have bottles and breast milk in the fridge but neither of us wants to bother with warming it up in the middle of the night when I can just feed her and be done with it."

"It's nice that he's stepping in and helping. Not many guys actually do that."

"Yeah, I got really lucky with Chase." She smiled and I looked away, hoping to hide some of the disappointment on my face as I thought about how great of a dad Noah was going to be. Only it wasn't with me.

"Are you okay?"

"Yeah." I took a deep breath and tried to gather my thoughts to keep from having a total meltdown. "I just keep trying to figure out what it's going to look like for us when Cindy has the baby and Noah has new responsibilities to handle. He's said that he wants me in the baby's life but Cindy has made it clear that she doesn't. It's been a little rough to figure out what my place is in all of this."

"When is she due?"

"She'll be 7 months in a few weeks. I only know because she scheduled her appointment for Valentine's Day and asked Noah if he wanted to grab dinner with her when they were done."

"Seriously? That's ballsy. And rude." Mia shook her head as I nodded along with her in agreement.

"Well, at least you still have some time before you guys have to decide on anything. Who knows, maybe Cindy will lighten up by then."

"Yeah, you never know." My mind drifted as I thought about what could change in the next few months as I held Rylee against me and wondered what Noah's baby's life would be like if I stayed in the picture. While I loved Noah and wanted to build a life with him I also had to take into consideration that I could complicate this innocent child's life simply by being a part of it. The last thing that I wanted was for this child to know drama and fighting because of me and their mom not being able to get along.

Twelve
Noah

It was almost four and Cindy was supposed to be meeting me at The Vine before we went to her ultrasound. I was thankful that Chase was back in the office this week and that today had been rather slow and uneventful for a Monday. I heard the door chime up front and glanced up to see blonde hair bouncing in a ponytail as the sun beamed in through the glass, obscuring my view of the actual person.

My heart beat faster as I excitedly waited for Jade to make it through the lobby but as soon as she stepped further into the room my heart sank when I saw it wasn't Jade. Standing before me was Cindy with hair as blond as Jade's, cut and styled the same exact way that Jade wears hers. I looked her over and noticed that she was wearing a pair of maternity bootleg jeans with a black lace shirt, similar to what Jade recently wore. The frumpy clothes she had been wearing since she moved here were now replaced with form-fitting clothes similar to Jade's style.

She grinned mischievously as she spun around in a slow circle, waiting for me to take it all in.

"What do you think?" She beamed as she held a hand up to her blonde hair and waited for my response. I tried to think of a quick response but the frown on my face gave it away before I could answer.

"You don't like it?" She threw her hand on her hip as she stared at me.

"I didn't say that I didn't like it. It's a lot to take in." I spoke cautiously as I had been doing more of the past few weeks. The back door opened as Chase came out, stopping in his tracks at the sight of her.

"Hey Chase," she purred, "you like my new look, don't you?" She pouted her mouth and batted her eyes as he glanced at me with a -what the fuck- kind of look on his face. I slightly shrugged my shoulders since I didn't have any fucking idea.

"Hey... look at that." He raised his eyebrows and avoiding saying anything more. "I need to talk to you about some of the recent orders, can you stop by my office tomorrow morning when you get in?"

"Sure thing." I nodded to him as he made his way back to the offices and shook his head as he left. Lucky bastard. "Well, we better get going so we're not late."

I grabbed my phone from the counter behind me and stuffed it in my pocket as I started walking towards the door.

"I'm not going anywhere until you tell me that you like my new look."

I spun around to see Cindy standing in the same spot, her arms folded across her chest as she stared at me, pissed off.

"What does it matter if I like it or not?" I took two steps toward her, pulling my shoulders back as I towered over her.

"Because it's important to me to know what you think." She looked shocked as she batted her eyes up at me.

"What I think is that it was stupid to bleach and color your hair when you're pregnant, but that's not really what you wanted to hear, now is it?" My mind was still trying to process why she would do this in the first place as I tried to fight the anger of the possible harm she put the baby in as she sat there with chemicals in her hair for hours while they stripped her brown hair to the almost platinum blonde it was now.

"You don't seem to have any issues with Jade having blonde hair." Her lips trembled as she said it, tears threatening to overflow from her eyes.

"Jade isn't pregnant with my child. And what Jade does to her look is not your concern. Maybe you should focus on taking care of yourself and this baby, and less on Jade." My tone was sharp as I turned around and stormed out the door, hearing the heavy footsteps as she followed behind.

I had never been to an ultrasound before and was thankful that she was far enough in the pregnancy that they didn't have to do much to get a good image of the baby on the screen. I sat back in the cold metal chair beside the bed she laid in, neither of us speaking to each other on the way over. The ultrasound tech squirted some gel on her belly and started moving the wand around as she adjusted a few things on her screen. I looked up at the tv mounted on the wall above me and felt my heart skip a beat when I saw the very recognizable image of a baby.

"There we go, there's your baby." The tech pointed to the screen as she flipped a switch and the sound of the heartbeat floated around us. My hands started sweating as I watched the baby move on the screen, a few big movements along with some small ones. I looked over at Cindy and stared at her pregnant belly in complete awe that my baby was inside of her and that I was getting to see it on the screen.

"When did you say your due date is?" The tech squinted her eyes as she leaned closer to the computer.

"April 7th." Cindy's eyes darted to the screen above my head as the tech wrote something down on a notepad beside her.

"Is there something wrong?" I asked cautiously as Cindy avoided looking at me.

"Not necessarily. We may have the wrong conception date in our system, I'm just looking back at other notes from her last visit."

I sat in silence, confused by what the tech was saying.

"Can you confirm the date of your last period?" She looked at Cindy, waiting for an answer.

"I, um, I don't remember. But I definitely got pregnant in July."

"Well the conception date listed does show a possible July or August conception date but the actual size of the fetus suggests that it was late August or early September. The baby is not measuring on track compared to the estimated gestational age based on the date of your last period."

My head was spinning as I struggled to make sense of everything.

"In plain English- what does that mean?" I leaned forward, resting my elbows on my knees as I looked up at the tech, hoping she would spell it out for me.

"It means that based on when she said she had her last period she should be around 7 months pregnant but the size of the baby is measuring around what we would see for someone who is 6 months pregnant."

Cindy let out a shaky breath as she stared at the tech who was gently using a towel to wipe the gel off of her stomach.

"I know when I got pregnant. It was over the Fourth of July when I came down here for the weekend." She cast a steely glance at me before turning her attention back to the tech. "Maybe we need a new tech who knows what she's doing and can accurately measure our baby."

I watched as a hardness came across the tech's face as she took in Cindy's accusation. While Cindy swore that she hadn't been with anyone else, part of me wondered if she hadn't been lying all along. We walked out with a handful of ultrasound photos and a follow-up appointment two weeks later to confirm the due date with the doctor based on how much the baby should grow during that period. It was either that they had the wrong conception date and Cindy wasn't as far along in the pregnancy as she claimed, or there was something wrong with the baby's growth. I chewed the inside of my cheek nervously as we drove back to The Vine in silence. The sky was gray as new clouds started moving in with the promise of a harsh winter storm.

I hopped out of the truck and made my way around to the passenger side to help Cindy down. It irritated me that she refused to drive herself to these appointments knowing damn well that she wasn't able to easily get in and out of my lifted truck. You would think that she would want to drive herself so she had the comfort and safety of her own car but she didn't.

"Hey, do you think I could hold onto one of the pictures from today?" I asked as I shoved my hands into my pockets and hoped that she would say yes without questioning why I wanted them. Her eyes lit up as she smiled and handed me the handful of pictures.

"Thanks, I can get them back to you soon. I just wanted to have one to show my parents." I lied straight-faced as she continued to beam.

"Go ahead and keep them, I know where to find them if needed."
She smiled as she ran a freshly manicured finger down my chest and swayed her hips as she walked to her car and left.

I rolled my eyes as I went back inside to check on things before heading out. When I walked inside I found Jade sitting at the bar with

Chase and Mia beside her as she cried. I rushed over, confusion on my face as I wrapped my arm behind her waist and looked at Chase. He gave me a tight smile as he stepped back from the counter, giving me some space.

"Jade, baby, what's wrong?" Her green eyes looked up to meet mine as fresh tears filled them.

"I lost it..," she stuttered before she started sobbing again. Mia wrapped her arms around her from the other side and whispered in her ear.

"Lost what?" I tried to keep my voice calm and supportive as I desperately waited for someone to clue me in on what was going on.

"The locket...." She sucked in jagged breaths. "The one my sister... gave me...before she..." Her voice cut off and I knew exactly what she was talking about and why she was so upset. She had shown me the locket a few times early on in our relationship and I knew how sentimental it was to her because it was the last thing her sister had given her before she was murdered. My heart squeezed tight in my chest as I gently turned her toward me and pulled her into my arms. I wrapped her as tightly as I could as she cried harder, Chase and Mia patting me on the back as they made their way out from behind the bar and carried Rylee to his office.

"Baby, I'm so sorry. We'll find it, I promise," I whispered in her ear as her body crumbled beneath me from the weight of losing the only thing in her life that was important to her.

Thirteen
Jade

The sun was almost completely set by the time I got to my apartment after leaving The Vine, having spent an hour there looking for the missing locket in Noah's office. I couldn't remember the last time I had seen it with everything being so crazy around me lately and panic had set in the moment I dumped everything out of my purse and still couldn't find it. I finally gave up and decided to go home and keep looking around my apartment, thankful that Noah was on his way to help me and would be bringing pizza and wine.

I climbed the last few steps and was walking toward my apartment when I looked up and saw someone standing with their back toward me, trying to open the door to the apartment next to mine. The apartment had been vacant for a few weeks after the incredibly loud party animal had finally been evicted. I was relieved to see him go and prayed that someone quiet was moving in instead.

I was about to say hi and introduce myself when the woman turned around and faced me before I could. My jaw dropped when I saw Cindy smiling at me, her hair a light blonde color, similar to mine.

"What are you doing here?" My confusion overrode my manners as I realized how rude I might have sounded after I said it. Her brows pulled together in response, a look of disappointment replacing the smile quickly.

"I'm moving into my new apartment, what does it look like?" She looked over her shoulder at the suitcase that sat behind her next to a few boxes stacked next to the window.

"You're moving in? To that apartment?" It was like my worst nightmare was coming true right before my very eyes.

"Yeah... that's why I'm holding the key." She rolled her eyes as she turned back to the doorknob and turned the key, opening the door to a furnished apartment that looked almost identical to mine. The only thing different was the bright colors I had used to make my space more personal, and that the layout was flipped to the opposite side. I peeled my eyes away from the apartment, trying to force myself to think about anything other than the woman standing in front of me that was trying to look like me and would now be living in the same apartment next door to me. My stomach dropped as a dark thought crossed my mind that she was actually trying to be me.

"What happened to your old apartment?" I leaned my shoulder against the small wall that separated our apartments and crossed my arms over my chest. Even with the thick scarf and heavy jacket, I felt a chill go through to my bones.

"I needed something bigger than a studio apartment for the baby. And I figured this would be perfect since Noah is over at your place half the time anyway, he would be close by to help with the baby. It was either this or move into his house. How crazy would that be?! The three of us living under one roof and raising a baby?" Her laughter reached a pitch that I'd never heard from her as she leaned her head back, laughing hysterically. I stayed watching her in disbelief as I heard footsteps approaching behind me.

"Hey, Noah! I was just telling Jade the exciting news about my new apartment. Did you want to come check it out?" She looked past me as I felt Noah's hand on my lower back, the tension in his body radiating toward me.

"Your new apartment?" His tone was stern as he kept his glare on her, his hand never leaving my body.

"Yeah, I was just about to get my stuff moved inside but you guys can come in and check it out if you want. Figured we'd be spending a lot of time here so you might as well make yourself at home right away." She smiled as if she didn't have a care in the world as Noah and I kept our stoic expressions. It felt like watching a horrific accident; you didn't want to see it but yet you couldn't look away.

"Maybe another time." Noah slowly pulled his hand away from my back as he turned his body toward me, blocking Cindy with his back.

"Let's get inside and eat before the pizza gets cold." His voice was quiet as he spoke, calming me from the meltdown I felt was coming. I nodded my head yes as my fingers felt around in my pocket until they found the keys and opened the door.

"Be careful moving stuff around and call downstairs if you need them to help you." His words were more of a warning than anything as he glanced over his shoulder at Cindy before gently leading me into the apartment with his hand on my lower back.

Once we were inside I heard the door click shut before Noah slid the deadbolt in place and sat the pizza down on the counter. We both stayed quiet as we worked to get out of the layers of clothes we were wearing, the tension around us thick.

"Did that seriously just happen?" I asked as I looked at Noah, hands on my hips. "Did she change her looks to look like me and then move into the apartment next door to me?! The same exact apartment as mine?!" My voice rose quickly, Noah wrapping me in a hug and holding me as he whispered in my ear.

"Watch what you say, these walls are super thin," he warned as he rubbed my back gently. "Remember how much we heard when that asshole next door was living there, she's going to be able to hear things just as easily."

"I can't believe it. It's like she's trying to take over my life. She would take you too if she could." I kept my voice low as I stepped back and looked up at Noah. The day had been long and draining with this taking the cake.

"She will never be you and she will never have me. Even if I wasn't with you, she still wouldn't have me." He leaned forward and kissed my forehead before grabbing my hand and leading me to the pizza.

We ate in silence as he worked to get the bottle of wine open, a much-needed treat for the night. The tension in the room subsided quickly as we cuddled on the couch and watched an old movie on the tv before getting the energy to look for the locket. My heart had been broken since I first noticed it was missing, part of me wondering if I had actually lost it or if my head was just too chaotic to remember where I had put it.

"I think it's officially lost," I muttered as I pushed myself up from being on my hands and knees looking under the bed with a flashlight. My body was sore from the constant stress I had been under lately, amplified by the weird positions I had been putting myself in trying to find the locket.

I closed my eyes as I leaned forward, slowly stretching as I bent down to touch my toes. My body tingled as I pushed myself deeper into the stretch, forcing the muscles to remember the yoga that I used to do daily. I smiled as I felt Noah come up behind me and gently grab my hips, lining himself up perfectly with my ass.

He slowly worked his hips as he teased me with a grinding motion, keeping his grip on me to keep me from falling over as I started laughing.

"Hey, I was trying to stretch!" I stood upright and playfully swatted at him as he moved in closer, a hungry look in his eye.

"Not to worry, I plan to stretch you as far as you can go." His voice was low and deep, pure sex dripping from every word.

"Oh really? Is that a threat or a promise?" I arched my eyebrow as I licked my bottom lip and locked eyes with him.

"Both." He studied me like a hunter would their prey, watching every move I made as he slowly pulled his T-shirt up and over his head. My eyes trailed over his muscular body as my fingers longed to reach out and touch him. I took a few steps backward, keeping my eyes on him as he moved towards me with determination. I felt my body change with every move he made, turned on by the way he looked at me. Suddenly the back of my legs bumped into the chair next to my dresser leaving me nowhere to go.

Noah's lips curled upward into a mischievous smile as he saw that I was trapped. My chest rose and fell heavily as I watched him creep closer, almost within reach. At last minute I ducked underneath his arm as he reached out to grab me and slid past him before he spun around and wrapped his arms around me, tickling my sides as he carried me over his shoulder to the bed. I giggled, his fingers continuing to tickle me as he climbed on the bed, dropping me on the soft mattress before climbing on top of me.

"You really thought you could get away that easy?" The smile on his face was one of the sexiest things about him as it lit up his hazel eyes.

"I gotta make you work for it, you can't just have me whenever you want," I teased as I blew a stray strand of hair off my face. His eyes got darker as he reached down and grabbed my hand, pulling it down to feel the bulge in his jeans.

"Baby, I will work you harder than you can handle," he growled as my fingers grabbed him through his jeans.

"Prove it." I licked my lips as I felt him twitch in my hand, my need to have him inside of me growing stronger.

He quickly rolled off me and kept his eyes on me as he took off his jeans and boxers. I let my eyes drift over to his massive cock as I lazily ran my fingers along the top of my bra. His fingers wrapped tightly around his shaft as he watched me, stroking up and down as my fingers pulled my bra down and traced over my pebbled nipple. My back arched in response, my breathing increasing to match his strokes.

"Fuck, Jade, you're gonna make me come just from watching you." He climbed up on the bed and pulled my leggings down before pushing my panties to the side and sliding a finger inside of me. I gasped at the welcomed intrusion, the wetness spreading as he moved his fingers inside of me. Within seconds my panties were gone and he was stroking himself while fingering me.

"I need you now, Noah," I begged as my body inched closer to orgasm.

"Now..," I panted as his fingers rubbed in circles over my clit. I reached up and ran my hands in his hair, pulling it as my body went over the edge, convulsing around his fingers.

"Fuck, you're so beautiful when you come." He pulled his fingers out as he slid himself inside of me, my body stretching to accommodate him. He stilled for a moment, allowing me time to adjust before he slowly rocked back and forth, closing his eyes as he increased his speed. I lifted my hips to let him in deeper, a groan from him in response as he plowed deeper inside of me. My legs wrapped around his waist as my hips ground into him, the headboard banging against the wall with each movement.

"We can't be too loud," I whispered as I nodded up toward the wall behind us. "Cindy is on the other side, remember?"

"Let her hear us. I want her to hear you moan as I fuck you, knowing that it will never be her."

His words stirred something deep inside me and a feeling of pride flowed through me as I realized how much he really did love me and that I didn't have to be jealous or insecure about Cindy.

He shifted his weight and lowered himself so he was rubbing against my clit. I could feel the pressure build as I watched him watching me. Harder. Deeper. Faster.

"Don't stop, right there..."

"That's it baby, come for me..."

"Noah...."

"Say my name baby, say it louder. Let her hear you as I make you come again. Say it baby," he coaxed as I screamed his name over and over, our bodies melting into a giant puddle of satisfied bliss as we climaxed together.

Fourteen
Noah

"How's Rylee doing? She's almost at the one month mark, right?" I leaned against the doorway to Chase's office, desperate to get my mind off of Cindy and the baby without much success.

"She's good, getting bigger every day. Mia is taking her for her wellness checkup today, but yeah, she'll be one month old on Saturday." He smiled proudly and my heart felt happy that Chase finally had the life he had always wanted.

"Does Mia still have the ultrasound pictures from when she was pregnant?" I scratched my head, feeling awkward for even asking. I still couldn't shake the thought that something might be wrong with the baby after the ultrasound tech said the baby wasn't measuring on track for how far along Cindy should be.

"Yeah, why?" He pulled his brows together as he leaned back in his leather chair and studied me.

I blew out a breath and ran a hand through my hair as I sat down in the chair across from him.

"The ultrasound tech said that the baby doesn't look like how a baby should look right now in the pregnancy."

"What does that mean?"

"Fuck if I know? She tried explaining it but Cindy got really defensive and kept arguing that she knew when she got pregnant."

"Did she think something was wrong with the baby?"

"She didn't say that, and she didn't seem to act like there was. We have another ultrasound at the end of the week, right before her 7 month prenatal appointment. They want to check the baby again and see if it's grown in the two-week period from the last one."

"So the baby is just measuring behind?" Chase ran a hand down his face before grabbing his cell phone and typing quickly while I talked.

"I guess so. The tech said that it looked like the baby would have been conceived late August or early September. Cindy is adamant that it was when she was down here for the Fourth of July which would make her close to seven months, the tech thinks the baby is closer to six months." I leaned back against the chair and waited while Chase did something on his phone.

"I know it might be hard to tell since you don't have a picture to compare it to, but this is Mia's from when she was six months pregnant with Rylee. Did the baby look like this?" He extended his cell phone to me, a Facebook post with the caption of baby Walker at 6 months. I got up and went to my office, grabbed the ultrasound photos from my desk drawer, and sat back down in front of Chase. I laid the photos on his desk as a smug smile crossed his face. He sat his phone down next to them as we craned our necks to look at them in comparison.

"I don't know, these look pretty much the same. Does it change much by seven months?" I asked as I stared at the pictures, trying to find anything that would help.

"Here, let me see. I think we posted monthly updates so there might be one from seven months." Chase pulled his cell phone in front of him and scrolled through posts until he found what he was looking for and sat his phone on the desk between us again.

We stared at the pictures, looking back and forth between the phone and the pictures, frustration evident when there was no apparent difference between the ultrasound photos. I pushed away from the desk and let out a heavy sigh as Mia walked into the office, balancing Rylee in her car seat on her arm.

"Hey, what's going on?" she asked as she looked down at the ultrasound pictures on Chase's desk then looking back and forth between us.

"It's a long story." I looked up at her apologetically, not having the energy to go through everything again.

"Humor me." Her eyes lit up as she looked to Chase knowing that he would give in and tell her.

"Cindy claims to be almost seven months pregnant but the last ultrasound shows the baby measuring around six months. We were trying to compare the ultrasound photos to the ones on Facebook of Ry." Chase smiled as Mia bent down to kiss him before setting the car seat down next to Chase. She leaned over the table and studied the ultrasound photos, picking one up to see it closer.

"It's hard to tell by just looking at these but the baby does look a little small. You can't go based on that though because you can't see the actual size of the baby, especially since it's zoomed in for the scan. But babies tend to plump up more around 7 months and this one isn't. When does she have her next prenatal appointment?"

"This Friday."

"Well, they should be checking her fundal height which should give a better idea of how far along she is."

"I'm sorry, her what?"

"Fundal height. It's a measurement from the top of the uterus to the pubic bone and it should be close to the number of weeks pregnant. For example, if she is close to 28 weeks pregnant, the fundal height should be around 26-30 centimeters. Are they doing another ultrasound as well?"

"Yeah, right before the checkup."

"That's good, I'm sure they'll be able to confirm everything then." She sat on the edge of the desk as Chase wrapped his arms around her waist from behind. "Why is Cindy having so many ultrasounds anyways? Is she high risk?"

"I have no idea, I just go where I'm told to go."

"You should ask and see. If she's high risk then it would be good for you to know what they're monitoring her for and be prepared."

"I guess I don't know much about all of this, do I?" I blushed as I looked away, embarrassed that I already felt like a failure as a father.

"It's all a learning process, my friend." Her eyes were sympathetic as she smiled. "Speaking of which, Cindy came by the house yesterday to ask me about labor and delivery. I hope she shared all of the gory details with you like she promised she would."

I could hear the teasing tone in her voice but my blood ran cold when I processed what she said.

"Cindy came by your house?"

"Yeah, she said that you told her to come talk to me." Mia paused as she looked at me, reading the expression on my face. "It wasn't a big deal, I didn't mind talking to her. I wish I would have had a heads up that she was coming, but it worked out better anyway when she helped me with Rylee."

"Mia, I NEVER told Cindy to come talk to you. I've never even talked to her about you guys." My heart started to race as I thought about Cindy alone with Mia and Rylee in the house.

"She made it seem like you suggested it. And then she said that us girls could spend some time talking about babies while you and Chase were at her apartment building the crib." Mia's eyes went wide as she looked back at Chase. "You guys weren't building the crib?"

"No, I was with Grant and Liam. We had baseball practice like usual. I'm sorry, I would have told you if I was going somewhere else Mia."

"Why would she lie to me? She acted like everyone was friends, I just thought maybe I wasn't that involved yet because I'm always at home with the baby."

"I don't know but I'm not liking the way things are going. Something's not right." I reached down and pulled my phone out of my pocket, sending a text message to Jade to see where she was. I knew she should be at work but with the way the day was going, anything was possible at this point.

"I agree, something doesn't feel right. I felt like something was off the other day when I saw that she had changed her hair to look like Jade." Chase's words struck a nerve as he said what I had been trying to deny all along. I shot him a stern look.

"What?" he asked, holding his hands up in defense. "I can't be the only one who finds it creepy that some random girl shows up out of the blue, knocked up, and within a few months she is literally doing everything that Jade does."

Mia and I sat in silence while Chase looked between us.

"Oh, come on! She works at the same place as Jade. Colored her hair the same color as Jade. Drives a red car like Jade. Started dressing like Jade. Slept with the same guy as Jade…. Am I missing the connection here?"

"And now she lives next door to Jade." I lowered my eyes as I heard their gasps. Chase was right, things were getting eerily similar.

"What the fuck?" Chase stared at me with complete shock on his face.

"Yeah, she just moved into the vacant apartment next door."

"You mean she is living right next door to Jade? As in they share a wall?" Mia's voice was shrill as she glanced down to make sure she hadn't woken Rylee up.

"Yes. Apparently, she told Jade that she needed something bigger than the studio she was in, and she thought it would be easier for me to help with the baby since I'm always at Jade's house when she's not at mine. And to top that off, she made a joke to Jade about how it was either live there or move in with me." I swallowed hard as I took in the gravity of the situation.

"Wow. I can't believe it. This is so creepy." Mia shuddered as she stood up next to Chase.

"Maybe I just need to talk to her? Like really talk to her and find out what the problem is?" I glanced down at my phone as a new message from Jade came through. I frowned as I read it.

"What's wrong?" Chase asked.

"Jade is on her way here."

"Why?" Mia questioned as she bent down to adjust the pacifier in Rylee's mouth as she started to stir.

"I don't know. Guess we'll see when she gets here."

"So what are we supposed to do now with Cindy?" Mia asked as she turned away from the baby who had fallen back asleep.

"What do you mean?"

"Well, I have to see her again soon, am I supposed to act like everything is normal and fine? Should I cancel on her?"

"Why are you seeing her again?"

I watched as Mia swallowed hard before answering.

"She's bringing something back that she borrowed."

My eyes narrowed as I waited for the bomb to drop.

"What did she borrow Mia?"

Her eyes were wide as she looked away, avoiding having to look at me. I stared at her while waited, clearing my throat to remind her that I was still there. Her eyes slowly lifted and made contact with mine.

"She has the photo album from our wedding. She said that she was working on a surprise gift for you and needed a recent picture of you. Those were the only ones that I had."

I closed my eyes and pinched the bridge of my nose as I heard footsteps down the hall as the door opened. I stood up and walked into the hall as Jade was heading toward me, tears on her face.

"Baby, what's wrong?" I pulled her tightly into me as she cried against my chest. She was still dressed for work but I noticed her badge that she used to get in and out of the building wasn't attached to her pocket like it usually was.

"They fired me." She sniffled as she pulled back and looked up at me, her eyes a light shade of gray.

"What? Why?" I stepped to the side as I heard Mia and Chase walk into the hallway behind us.

"I was accused of bullying and harassment, creating a hostile work environment, and showing favoritism with other employees."

My jaw clenched knowing who was responsible for this.

"That's bullshit." I shook my head knowing that there was nothing that I could say that would make this any better.

"I tried talking to them but they said that they have to take the accusations seriously and that they had noticed the tension between Cindy and I. Given that she was the one who went to them to file the report, they claim they had no choice other than to fire me."

"Jade, I'm so sorry." Mia came around from behind me and wrapped her in her arms as Chase and I looked at each other. I was furious as I thought of the things I planned to say when I saw Cindy.

"I'll be back." I looked straight at Chase, seeing Jade's head whip up from Mia's shoulder as I stalked off down the hallway.

"Noah, where are you going?" Jade called behind me as the door closed, silencing her pleas for me to come back.

It was after five which meant that Cindy should be home by now given that the bank closed every day at four. I veered in and out of traffic, my anger building the closer I got. As I made my way up the stairs I felt my pocket vibrate and pulled out my phone to see a message from Chase confirming that Stacy would close up tonight and they were taking Jade back to their house. I shoved my phone back into my pocket as I reached Cindy's door, pounding loudly with my fist. Her car was downstairs in the parking lot which meant she was here. I waited a few seconds before pounding again, my hand slipping when the door flung open, Cindy's eyes wide as she stood on the other side.

"Noah, what's wrong?" Her voice was high, eyes filled with concern as she stepped back and allowed me to come inside. I slammed the door behind me as I stood in front of her, glaring.

"What the fuck is wrong with you?" I towered over her, looking down with fury on my face as I watched her reaction.

"What are you talking about? Maybe I should ask what the fuck is wrong with you?" She stepped away and walked over to sit on the couch, plopping her feet up on the old wood coffee table in front of her.

"You got Jade fired. That's what's wrong."

"I had nothing to do with that." She arched her eyebrow and I immediately wanted to wipe that smug look off of her face.

"Really? Because it seems like you were the one who filed the report claiming that she was bullying and harassing you."

"I didn't file a report. I completed the required paperwork for my thirty-day performance evaluation that asked me about my experience. I was honest like they asked me to be." She crossed her arms over her chest and stared at me.

"Jade has never bullied you and you know it."

"Yeah well, she wasn't the most pleasant person to work with either."

"So you got her fired because you don't like her?"

"She got herself fired because she doesn't know how to be nice to other people."

"You seriously have issues. If you think that you can move to a small town like this and treat people that way, you've got another thing coming. Whatever this bullshit act is that you have going- just stop now. I don't have time for it and quite frankly, I'm not interested."

"So what? You're just going to walk away and abandon me and your unborn child for some girl that's an easy lay?" She stood up and walked toward me, pure evil on her face.

"I never said that I was walking away from my child, I said that you need to learn how to treat people if you want to make it in this town. And trust me, Jade wasn't the easy lay." I looked her up and down as my eyes lingered over her stomach. Her face turned a dark shade of red and for a moment I expected to see smoke come out of her ears.

"You really need to have more respect for the woman who is carrying your child." She pulled her shoulders back as she stepped closer.

"I never asked you to." My blood was boiling and it took everything inside of me to remember that she was a woman. You don't put your hands on a woman. Never put your hands on a woman.

Within seconds she was on me, wrapping her arms around my neck as she forced her lips onto mine. I quickly stepped back, pushing her away with my arm as I glared at her.

"What the hell was that?" My eyes narrowed, her face falling at my reaction.

"I don't know why you keep trying to fight this thing between us, Noah. We're going to be together for the rest of our lives, bound together by this baby. It just makes sense that we should be together. You know, for the baby."

"Is that what this is all about? Us being together?"

"It just makes sense that a child should see their mother and father together. In love." Her last word fell on her lips as a whisper.

"Cindy, I'm not in love with you. I'm having a child with you but nothing more. Do you understand that?" I took a deep breath and watched as she slowly started to calm down.

"But you could love me, if you just tried." She looked up at me under thick lashes, her eyes pleading with mine.

"I'm in love with Jade, Cindy."

"So you think. But she's not the person you think she is. I've seen a side of her that's cold and vengeful. You don't want someone like that in your life. I could make you so much happier than she ever could." She rubbed a hand over her stomach as she stepped closer.

"I'm not here to talk about my relationship with Jade. I'm here to talk about us and set boundaries in place. If we're going to try to raise this baby together then we need to respect each other and stick to those boundaries. Okay?"

She slowly nodded her head yes, taking another step forward as I took a step back.

"My relationship with Jade will remain private. You will leave her alone and stop showing up at Mia's house unexpectedly. If and when I want to have you involved in my personal life, I will let you know. Once it gets closer to the baby coming, we'll sit down again and talk about what things will look like at that point. Until then you can keep me updated on doctor's appointments and I'll do my best to be there." I looked sternly at her, waiting for her to object but she didn't.

"Okay." She pursed her lips and folded her arms over her chest as I nodded my head and walked out the door, slamming it behind me.

THE CRADLE WILL FALL

Fifteen
Jade

I rolled over and found the sun filtering into the room through the sheer curtains, Noah's dark hair looking lighter from the warm glow it cast on the pillow. It felt weird to get up and not have a job to get ready for. I let out a deep breath as I rolled over and slid out of bed, making my way to the kitchen to start a pot of coffee. It was still early but I was restless and had struggled to stay asleep most of the night, even with having Noah next to me. Usually having him in bed next to me would calm me but for some reason, nothing could calm the uneasy feeling that seemed to be lingering around.

I sat on the soft rug on the floor and closed my eyes as I slowly reached up and stretched, taking in a deep breath and slowly exhaling. My body was stiff and rigid, fighting every stretch as I pushed myself further into them. If I could force my body to give in and relax, maybe my mind would do the same. My eyes were still closed when I heard footsteps down the hall as Noah made his way to the living room.

"Maybe I should start staying over more often if this is the view in the morning."

I heard the sound of the coffee pot as he sat it back down and looked over my shoulder to see him shirtless leaning against the counter as he sipped his coffee while watching me. I chuckled as I turned back around and focused on the stretch, spreading my legs further apart in a wide V in front of me as I laid my torso flat against the rug and extended my arms above my head.

"Then again, maybe I'll just stay at my own place so I don't have to worry about walking around with blue balls every time you decide to do yoga," he joked as he walked past me and sat on the couch.

"Very funny." I laughed as I finished the stretch before I got up and sat next to him. "You never have blue balls so don't start acting like you do now."

"See for yourself." He held his coffee cup in one hand while he pulled the waistband of his sweats out so I could look inside. Feeling a bit rowdy I reached my hand inside and grabbed him, feeling him jerk in response as the coffee sloshed in the mug.

"Hmm, not blue." I bit my lip as I pulled my hand away and stood up, swaying my hips as I walked to the kitchen to look for something to make us for breakfast.

I was leaning against the refrigerator door when I felt Noah come up behind me and wrap his arms around my waist. A smile crossed my face as I felt the bulge in his pants against my butt, loving that there was rarely ever a moment that he wasn't turned on around me. He ran a hand up my stomach and over my chest as he kissed my neck. I closed my eyes as a whimper escaped, my body finally starting to relax.

"What do you want for breakfast?" I asked with my eyes still closed, enjoying his hands as they roamed my body.

"You."

I giggled as I playfully bumped him with my butt, his hands quickly grabbing my hips and holding me in place.

"You always want me," I teased. "What kind of food do you want?" I closed the door to the refrigerator and turned around to look at him. He slowly backed me up against the cold steel of the fridge as he pinned me against it and leaned his body on mine. His eyes changed and I watched with curiosity as he looked at me, searching for something.

"Move in with me." His words were soft and full of sincerity.

"What? You don't want me to live with you, it's too soon." My head was spinning as I thought about what he was asking me. I loved Noah but there wasn't any way that he was serious about us moving in together right now with everything going on.

"There's nothing that I want more, Jade. I want to wake up every morning to your beautiful face, and fall asleep every night inside of you."

"You're such a romantic." I playfully rolled my eyes at him knowing that I loved being with him more than anything. Maybe that was what had kept us together this long? Incredible, mind-blowing sex that neither of us could get enough of.

"I never claimed to be romantic, just good in bed. And we both know there haven't been any complaints in that department." His eyes danced wildly as they watched me squirm beneath him as his finger ran down my stomach and over my hip before reaching down and spreading his palm across my pussy.

"No complaints indeed," I whispered as my body froze beneath his touch.

"Then move in with me. Please." He leaned closer and lightly kissed my neck as his hand continued to play with me over my thin pajama pants. "We practically already live together, we sleep over at each other's place every other night."

"But, Noah," I murmured, ready to give in.

"No buts, just move in with me." His hand moved as he dipped it inside of my pajamas, moving my panties out of the way as he worked two fingers inside of me. My body came alive as he slid in and out of me, kisses creating a trail of fire as he planted them across my shoulder and down my chest.

"Are you using sex to try to lure me to the dark side?" I panted as my body responded to his touch, my back arched as my legs started to tremble.

"Whatever it takes to get you there," he whispered in my ear as his fingers rubbed my clit harder, my body on the verge of orgasm.

"Yes! Yes! Yes!" I screamed as my body gave in, his fingers clutched by the tight convulsions as I spasmed against him. I leaned my head against his chest as he chuckled, my hands wrapped around his neck.

"You cheat." I grinned as I said it knowing that he was feeling pretty cocky about it.

"Hey, you said yes, there was no cheating on my end."

"I was lost in the moment, I didn't know what I was saying yes to." I looked up at him with playful eyes, surprised to see the love reflected back at me in his.

"Well, if you move in with me, I can promise to give you an orgasm every morning and two every night." He ran a finger across my cheek as his eyes pleaded with mine.

"Okay," I sighed.

"Okay what?" He tilted his head as he waited for my response.

"I'll move in with you." I let out a nervous breath. "But I want a minimum of four orgasms a day." I quirked a brow as I tried to hide my smile.

"Done." His lips were heavy on mine as he kissed me, lifting me into his arms before carrying me back to the bedroom.

<u>Sixteen</u>
Noah

"You all done there, champ?" I leaned across the table and handed Liam a napkin to wipe his mouth as he finished his last bite of cheeseburger. While cheeseburgers weren't originally on the menu at The Vine, they had been a consistent item shortly after Grant had quit his job over a year ago and needed to feed Liam after school. For a while, they were living with Grant's mom so she could help take care of Liam while Grant was at work but after he quit his demanding job and took a position teaching PE at Liam's school, he decided it was time to be out on their own again. The last month The Vine had seen a significant increase in cheeseburger sales which confirmed Grant had in fact moved out.

"Yeah, I'm stuffed." He pushed the plate toward the center of the table and leaned back the way I'd seen his dad do over the years. I let out a soft chuckle when I noticed how much Liam was a spitting image of his dad and quietly wondered how much of me my own child would have in them. Would people think the same thing? Would they see the same little quirks and traits in my kid that they saw in me when I was little?

"Good. You know we have other stuff than just burgers and fries, right?" I eyed him suspiciously, knowing his answer before it came out.

"I'm good. I'm a meat and potatoes kind of man."

I leaned back in my chair as laughter forced its way through my body, filling the silence around us. Liam smiled, completely proud that his response got such a rise out of me.

"I'm sorry, I won't push the other stuff on you anymore. I didn't know you had become such a distinguished man with set tastes," I joked, still laughing.

"I'm almost eleven, so that makes me one year closer to being a man." He sat upright in his chair and attempted to puff his chest out while I looked away and chewed my lip to keep from laughing.

"Hey, um, Noah, can I ask you a question? You know, man to man?" He raised his eyebrows as he said the word man.

"Sure, what's up?"

"My dad said that you're having a baby."

"Yeah, that's true." I nodded my head while I waited for him to ask his question.

"But it's not with Jade, it's with another girl."

"That is also true." My brow furrowed as I wondered what he was trying to ask.

"So you love Jade and you guys live together now, but you're having a baby with another woman. Is she carrying your baby because Jade can't?" He titled his head at me in confusion.

I blew out a breath and shifted in my seat, wishing Grant was out here with us instead of talking to Chase in his office. How was I supposed to talk about this with Liam? I had no clue what he knew and didn't know about girls or sex or one night stands but I sure as hell didn't want to be the one to teach him any of it.

"No Liam, she's having my baby because there was a night where we were together, but Jade and I were broken up."

"So, if you like a girl and you want to hang out with her, does that mean that you have to have sex with her? Like if she wants to be your girlfriend, do you have to have sex?"

"No, you don't ever have to have sex with anyone that you don't want to." I ran a hand down my face feeling like this conversation was starting to get out of control and heading in a direction that Grant wouldn't be happy about.

"What's going on Liam? Where are these questions coming from?"

"Well, there are these two girls at school that I really like and my buddy Luke said that he heard that they both like me too and that they BOTH said that they want to be my girlfriend. I just don't know that I'm ready for all of this." He sighed and leaned forward, resting his elbows on the table as he looked at me. "You gotta help me, Noah, you know what it's like to have all the ladies wanting you."

I ran my hand across my face, attempting to hide my laughter without success. Liam scowled at me before I saw the corners of his mouth twitch before giving in to a full-blown smile on his face. Soon we were both bent over laughing so hard that Liam would snort and send us further into hysterics. I felt a hand clap my shoulder and turned to see Grant and Chase standing behind me, smiling.

"What's so funny?" Grant asked as he spun a chair around and straddled it backward.

"You know, the usual girl problems." Liam waved his hand dismissively before whispering something to Chase who had taken the empty seat next to him.

"Oh really?" Grant eyed me as his tone changed, forcing me into another bout of laughter.

"Relax, I've got this." I patted his knee as I turned my attention back to Liam.

"Alright little man, here's how you solve your problem. First, you decide which of the girls you like the most and you make an effort to find out if she likes you too. Second, you don't try to date two girls at the same time. It will be nothing but trouble. And third, you don't wait to see which one wants you before you decide which one you want. That's the pussy way of doing things and everyone involved deserves better than that. Treat the girl with respect and remember that you both need to be in agreement before even talking about sex." I winked as I saw Grant fling his arms up in the air beside me.

"Wait- What?!" His eyes narrowed at me as Liam sunk further in his chair and Chase tucked his chin in to hide his laughter. "What the fuck kind of conversation did I just walk in on?"

"You might want to watch the language." I gritted between my teeth, nodding toward Liam, hoping it would lighten Grant's mood.

"Really? From the guy who just told my son not to be a pussy?"

"Alright, fair enough." I looked over at Liam and he nodded subtly. "Liam here was confused about my situation with Jade and Cindy. He wanted to make sure that just because someone is his girlfriend, that it doesn't mean that they have to have sex. I was just confirming that he doesn't have to have sex if he doesn't want to. And," I looked sternly at Liam, "it's something that he should wait for until he's ready. I get that he's a meat and potatoes kind of man now, but sex is a huge deal and it can have serious consequences with adult responsibilities."

"Like you and Cindy." Liam smiled proudly.

"Yup. So if you don't want to be a father at your age, you need to really think about it before you start having sex. Don't be afraid to talk to us, we have plenty of years of experience between us so we're pretty much experts at sex and relationships."

Laughter erupted around me as Liam shook his head and walked away, heading to the gated-in patio out back. I was thankful that the mood had shifted and Grant no longer looked like he wanted to murder me.

"Sorry about that, he caught me off guard by asking and I wasn't sure how you would want me to answer."

"It's fine, the kid has to learn at some point, and honestly it's not like he won't hear the town talk about how you've slept with everyone here." Grant nudged me with his elbow.

"Those days are over my friends. I'm a one-woman man now." I leaned back and laced my fingers behind my head.

"Yeah? So which woman are you with? The one you moved in with you or the one you knocked up?" Chase joked though I could hear the underlying truth in it.

"Jade is the girl for me. And yeah, Cindy will be there because of the baby, but that's it. I've already talked to her and reset expectations."

"I don't think it's going to be that easy. I think Cindy wants more and going by what I have seen from her so far, I don't see her stopping until she gets it." Chase reached forward and pointed at me. "You need to be careful with her, there's something about her that I just don't trust."

"I agree with Chase. Sorry, but I think you have bigger issues with her than you think."

I didn't want to admit that they were both right but I hadn't been able to stop thinking about what had happened after I went to her apartment to talk to her. The way she looked at me when she tried to convince me that I could love her the way that I loved Jade had made me uncomfortable. But the way she didn't even flinch when I accused her of trying to be Jade made me even more uncomfortable. My palms started sweating as I ran them down the front of my jeans.

"It's fine, I can handle it." I looked between them feeling their doubts cast upon their face, a reflection of what I felt inside.

"This is real life, Noah. It's not all rainbows and orgasms. It's not the bullshit games that you used to play with women. This is an innocent child involved and the possibility that you could lose the first woman you've ever loved. If that doesn't mean something to you then I don't know what will." Chase shook his head as he stood up and walked off to the back offices.

I hung my head and let out a sigh as I glanced over at Grant. I knew that Chase was right but I wasn't ready to admit to myself so it felt like a fucking attack coming from him.

"What? You don't have any salt to add to the wound? Any jokes about how I'll likely fail as a father?" I pushed knowing that I was purposely trying to start a fight so I would have something else to focus on.

"Oh I have plenty, but I'll save it for another time." He pinned me with a look that told me everything was about to get real.

"Noah, stop acting like an immature little asshole and figure out how to do the right thing for everyone. If you love Jade and you want to be with her, then make some grand gesture."

"I thought I did by begging her to move in?"

"Really? That was your big gesture? Asking her to move in with you when you guys are practically living together anyway?"

"It felt like a big step." I let out a heavy breath as I took in his words.

"It was, but if you want to keep her in your life you have to do something even bigger. You have to assure her that she's the one that you want in your life, that nothing else will ever take your love from her. Things are going to change, and soon. That baby will be here before you know it and when it gets here, your life is going to be completely changed. You're going to constantly be with Cindy and that's going to make Jade feel insecure and probably a little jealous. That baby is going to take so much of your time and attention that you won't have as much to give Jade. She's going to pick up on it and your absence will be felt by her, whether you acknowledge it or not. What we're saying is you need to be working on your relationship with Jade right now and fuck everything else. If you can't get to a new level with Jade that makes her feel like she is wanted and needed in your life, you're going to end up losing her when the baby comes."

"So what am I supposed to do?"

"I don't know. I can't tell you what to do. You're the only one who can figure out what you want from your relationship with her. Maybe it's asking her to marry you. Maybe it's talking about the future and letting her know that you want to someday have kids with her. I really don't know."

"That's it! That's what I'm going to do!" I slammed my fist down on the table excitedly as my eyes looked up at Grant, thankful that he talked me into what I needed to do.

"What? What are you going to do?" His forehead wrinkled as his brow arched.

"I'm gonna ask her to marry me."

Seventeen
Jade

"So what are you going to do now for a job?" Mia asked as she cut the last few pieces of cucumber and tossed it in the salad bowl on the island.

"I told her she could work at The Vine until you get back from maternity leave." Noah snuck up behind me and wrapped his arms around me. I leaned back against him, inhaling the light scent of his cologne as I slightly tilted my head toward his neck out of habit.

"You better be careful, I'm not afraid to clear this island and eat you for dinner, Ms. Alyson." He nipped at my ear as he kept his whisper low enough for only me to hear. I felt a blush creep up my neck as I gently pushed my hips back and rubbed my ass against him. His fingers dug into my hips as I heard a sharp intake of air as I looked playfully over my shoulder and bit my lip.

"Don't make promises you can't keep, Mr. Wilder." I pulled my bottom lip in between my teeth before smiling and releasing it. He softly reached up and ran the pad of his thumb over it, a look of desire on his face. I heard a low grumble from deep inside his chest before Chase opened the sliding glass door and rolled his eyes at us.

"Seriously? Can't you guys keep your hands off each other for two minutes?" he grumbled as he poked his head in.

"Stop, it's cute," Mia teased over her shoulder before turning toward him to wash a carrot in the sink. "There was a time when you couldn't keep your hands off of me."

"I remember quite vividly. And I believe that might be how miss Rylee got here." He nodded to the playpen in the corner of the living room where she slept peacefully.

"Those were the days," Mia whispered under her breath as she turned back to the island and gave me a sad look.

Chase slid the door open and sat the barbecue tongs on the counter behind him before grabbing Mia from behind and tickling her as she giggled.

"6 days. 9 hours. 23 minutes," he said loud enough for everyone to hear. Mia looked up over her shoulder and frowned at him.

"Until what?" she asked.

"Until it's been six weeks and you're officially cleared. Then I plan to give Noah some baby practice while they watch Ry for us so I can spend the entire night and the next morning making love to you because damn if six weeks isn't a hell of a long time to go without being with you." He planted soft kisses along her shoulder as she giggled and blushed.

"Come on Noah, this meat isn't going to cook itself. Grab some beers and make yourself useful." Chase grabbed the tongs from the counter and turned to head back outside, smacking Mia firmly on the ass on his way out. Noah laughed and shook his head as he grabbed the beers and followed him. After the sliding door was closed I pulled out the barstool and sat across from Mia while she cut up the carrot and tossed it in the salad.

"You guys are as cute as you were when you first started dating."

"Thanks, I feel very insecure about everything right now and keep thinking that he's going to get bored and start looking for someone else already."

"Are you kidding? You guys are married. He loves you..."

She sat down the knife and planted her palms flat on the island as she looked at me. She didn't have to say the words for me to see that she was terrified that he would cheat on her like her ex-husband had.

"Mia, he's not Damian. He adores you. And Rylee. And he probably would have taken you here on this island if we weren't here," I joked watching the smile cross her face. "Trust me, I don't think he's going to be too strict with that countdown." I laughed and felt relieved when she joined me.

"I know he loves me and he loves Rylee but I don't know that he still wants me. My body isn't the same and honestly, I'm so exhausted from the baby that I don't know that I would even want to have sex. What if I disappoint him?" She extended her arms out and shrugged.

"Do you want to know what I see when I look at you?"

"Probably not." She rolled her eyes as I tossed a discarded carrot top at her.

"Well too bad because I'm going to tell you anyway. I see a woman who has gained so much confidence in the past two years. I see a woman who is strong. Who is determined. Who has a beautiful body that has some majorly sexy new curves. And seriously, I'm not sure that Chase knows that you have a face anymore because every time I see him, he's staring at your boobs." I looked pointed at her chest as she looked down at the sweater that was pulled tight against her chest.

"He does not!"

"He does. It might be a new fetish for him, who knows." I shrugged and laughed as she swatted at me, the blush creeping up her face.

"Don't be so hard on yourself, Mia, he still loves you and I can tell that he's still very much turned on by you." I smiled to reassure her as she smiled back at me.

"I guess I can say the same for you and Noah?" She called over her shoulder as she opened the fridge and pulled out a tray with cut lettuce, tomato, and onions.

"Yeah, things are good between us. For now." I sighed and lowered my head as I picked at the magenta-colored nail polish that was starting to chip.

"What's that supposed to mean?" She sat the tray on the island beside the salad before reaching back in to grab a bowl of potato salad.

"I don't know. I guess things aren't necessarily doomed so to speak but I can't sit here and expect that things will stay the same when Cindy has the baby. I know that things are going to change, I just don't know how much. Maybe instead of taking steps forward, I should be taking steps back."

"Are you regretting moving in with him?" She pulled out the other barstool and sat next to me, leaning back to check on Rylee before getting comfortable. I glanced out the kitchen window and saw Noah and Chase, their heads back laughing at something while their breath formed clouds of smoke in front of them from the cold air. It felt weird to me that they wanted to barbecue in the middle of winter but apparently, Chase was in the mood and didn't care how cold it was.

"I don't necessarily regret it but I also haven't bothered terminating my lease yet either. Which is stupid because I can't afford to keep paying rent when I don't have a job." I blew out a frustrated breath and looked at her. "I don't want to end up being the roommate that he has sex with because it's convenient and he's too nice to kick me out after his life with Cindy starts when the baby gets here."

Mia's face fell, mimicking the way my heart dropped to my stomach after I said it. I had been questioning everything for weeks now but I hadn't been honest with myself about what I was actually afraid of. I had fallen in love with a man who was now about to fall in love with someone else. His child.

It was a different kind of love and I knew that, but it would be stupid of me to think that he could handle everything at the same time. There was no way that he could still be with me and grow in our relationship while also devoting time to his child. That meant that when the child got here, our relationship would be cemented where it was and I wasn't sure that it would ever be enough for me.

"The baby will definitely change things, I'm not going to lie. It's going to be hard and he's going to be focused on the baby and nothing else for a while. But if you can be patient and supportive until he gets a hold on everything, I really do think you guys can have an awesome relationship. Have you guys talked about the future? Getting married? Having kids of your own?"

"No, it all felt like it was too soon to talk about that stuff then bam, Cindy shows up and now it feels weird to talk to him about having a kid of our own when he's having one with someone else." I played with the forks on the table in front of me, not ready to make eye contact with Mia. Her hand reached over and softly touched my arm.

"Jade, you're not your mom. It's okay to let your guard down and be happy with someone. Her past is not your future."

My eyes shot up towards hers as tears filled them, threatening to spill over. My mind raced as it thought about what she said, no time to respond to her as I saw the guys walking to the door with plates full of meat in their hands. I felt like a deer in the headlights as Noah looked at me, his smile immediately replaced with concern when he saw the look on my face. I slid off the barstool and rushed off to the guest bathroom, locking the door as I slid down it and held my face in my hands.

A few minutes later I heard a soft knock at the door.

"Hey, is everything okay?" Noah's asked quietly. I stood up and glanced in the mirror before I opened the door.

"Yeah, I just needed a moment."

His eyes searched mine as he leaned against the doorway and crossed his arms.

"You sure you're okay?"

"Yeah, I'm good." I forced a smile hoping he would take it and let it be. He quirked a brow as he kept studying me. I let out a deep breath as I dropped my shoulders and looked at him.

"It's not a big deal, really. It's not important. Let's get back out there before dinner is cold."

I went to step in front of him when he reached an arm out, stretching it across the doorway to block me. His hazel eyes darkened as he watched me, the fabric of his hoodie stretching tight across his muscular chest.

"Jade, don't you know by now? If it involves you, then it's important."

There were genuine love and sincerity reflected in his voice which killed me knowing that I had to end this thing between us, breaking both of our hearts in the process.

Eighteen
Noah

"You've been awful quiet tonight since dinner, you sure you don't want to talk about what's bothering you?" I reached across the middle console of the truck and placed a hand on Jade's leg as I focused on the back road that would eventually lead to an old abandoned farm with acres of land around it. I loved coming out here and just lying in the bed of the truck, looking at the stars, and forgetting the rest of the world even existed.

"Yeah, I've just been doing some thinking."

Her head leaned back against the headrest while she looked out the window into the darkness that surrounded us.

"I'm here if you want to talk, you know that. Right?"

She had been acting so different with me tonight and I couldn't put my finger on what had happened while she was inside with Mia. She was pulling away and the thought of losing her was starting to feel more real. Nothing had worked to get her to talk to me and I felt desperate to try to get through to her. I needed her more than I needed air at this point.

She nodded her head in agreement as she continued to stare out the window, her hand reaching up to wipe away a tear as it slid down her cheek. I sighed heavily as I pulled the truck over on the side of the road and turned in my seat to look at her.

"Baby, please talk to me. Something is wrong, I can clearly see it on your face." I reached over and wiped another tear as it fell. My chest felt tight and something told me that I wasn't going to like what she was about to say.

"I think we should stop seeing each other." Her voice was stern as her lip trembled, her eyes still focused on the darkness outside the truck. I closed my eyes and leaned my back against the cold door. This can't be happening. Not now. Not when everything was heading in the right direction. Suddenly I felt the weight of the world on my shoulders, the happiness I had felt earlier when I bought the engagement ring dissipating. I opened my eyes and looked at her as she slowly turned toward me, tears rolling down her face.

"What brought this on?" I asked calmly, trying my best to keep the raw emotion I felt out of my voice.

"There's a lot of change coming, and soon. I don't think that our relationship is in a place to withstand that level of change."

"I think that we can push through whatever comes our way if we're in this for the right reasons. I know I am." I watched her face fall and felt bad at the insinuating tone that made its way through.

"Do you really think that we're in a place to handle moving in together and a few months after that, you having a baby with another woman?" She pulled her brows together and frowned.

"I do. Because there's nothing that I want more than you, Jade."

"You say that now but a baby changes everything, Noah. Look at how much it changed Chase and Mia-- and they're married. It still had a major impact on their relationship and they were a lot further along in their relationship when she got pregnant than we are."

"So what? Do you want to get married? Have a baby? What is it that's missing that would make you feel like our relationship is where you want it to be?"

"Time." Her eyes pierced mine as the word hung in the air between us.

"Jade, I know that having the baby come soon is scary. I'm not gonna lie, I'm freaking the fuck out about it. But just because I'm having a baby doesn't mean that I can't have you too. I can love you and be with you while also being a dad to a baby. Every relationship has its ups and downs, Jade, but if we give up every time things get a little hard there would never be a lasting relationship. People would just bounce from one relationship to another, never planting any actual roots to build something lasting with someone else."

I watched as her chest fell and she lowered her eyes. Suddenly I knew what it was really about.

"Jade, is all of this about us and me having a baby? Or is it about your childhood and watching your mom run from every relationship she ever had before things got too complicated?"

She lowered her head into her hands and I watched her body shake as she cried. I slid over as close as I could to the middle console and reached over and grabbed her, pulling her into me as I tried to comfort her.

"You don't have any idea of what my childhood was like or what relationships I've been in." Her breath was ragged from crying but her words were sharp with anger.

"I know what you've told me, I can't be faulted for not knowing more if you don't open up to talk to me," I spoke softly and gently to avoid sounding like a total asshole. I knew from the few times that we had talked about her childhood that her mother had constantly bounced from relationship to relationship, getting what she could from the guy before moving on when they wanted a commitment. Jade had always said that's why she is as wild and free-spirited as she is now, she never learned how to actually settle down and stick with something or someone. I felt her pull away from me as she sat back against her seat and wiped her face with both hands.

"Well we're talking now and I'm telling you that I don't think this is going to work. We should cut our losses and move on."

"Is that what you want?" My stomach churned as I waited for her answer, praying that she would come to her senses.

"Yes."

I blew out a deep breath as I turned forward in my seat and started the truck. I glanced in the rearview mirror out of habit, knowing that no one ever came down this road that dead-ended at the abandoned farm. As I was about to pull forward I caught a glimpse of a car parked off in the distance behind us that I hadn't seen when we first pulled up. It was too dark to see it clearly, let alone confirm who was in the car. Frustrated enough with how the night had ended I sped off in the opposite direction, not giving a fuck about who was in the car.

Nineteen
Jade

Can I get you anything else?" I slid the receipt onto the table next to the full glasses of water as the elderly couple shook their head no and continued with their meal. It was my second day working at SlowMo's and I was slowly starting to adjust to waitressing again. I reached up and adjusted my ponytail as I stood behind the register waiting for another table to come in and keep me occupied. It was slow for a Friday but then I found that it was slow pretty much every day in Haven Brook compared to the fast-paced environment of the night clubs I worked at when I lived in Boston.

It had been two days since I saw Noah after he dropped me off at my apartment and didn't look back. I saw the hurt in his eyes when I told him that I wanted to end things between us. I knew that it would hurt him but I didn't expect that it would kill me. All night I kept trying to convince myself that it was the right thing to do. If you love someone, let them go. I guess I just thought that he would put up more of a fight. When he didn't, my heart broke even harder and I started to question whether he was actually as invested in the relationship as I was.

The bell chimed as the front door swung open, a huge bouquet of red roses blocking the face of the man delivering them as he made his way to the counter. A sudden feeling of excitement burst through me when I thought they might be from Noah and there might still be a chance to save the relationship that I swore I didn't want.

"Can I help you?" I asked as I tilted my head to the side to see his face behind the flowers.

"Um yeah, I have a delivery for..... oh golly, the name was right here. Hold on a minute." He tried to hold the massive bouquet in one hand as he fumbled with a clipboard with the other. I reached over and grabbed the vase from him, sitting it on the counter beside him. He smiled up at me as he used both hands to hold the clipboard, scrolling down the page with his finger until finding the name he was looking for.

"Arlene. Arlene Bennett." He smiled and raised his eyebrows as he waited for me to confirm who she was. I let out a disappointed sigh as I leaned back and called for Arlene. A few minutes later she came up to the front, a hand covering her mouth when she saw the display of roses on the counter. I signed for the flowers and watched as he waved and walked out the door.

"Oh my goodness, these are just beautiful." She looked up at me, beaming, as she lightly ran her hand across the fragrant flowers.

"They are." I smiled and watched as she found the card tucked inside a heap of baby's breath. She pulled it out and a beautiful smile spread across her face as she read it, clutching it to her chest and looking up at me when she was done.

"You know, Joe has never missed a single Valentine's Day since we've been together. Every year there's a different flower that he chooses for the bouquet. It's been a while since he's done roses, but this year is our 25th anniversary and roses were the very first flower he ever gave me."

I loved hearing love stories that had happy endings and had learned a lot about Arlene and Joe's love story through Mia as she spent time getting to know the father she never knew about until a few years ago. I had totally spaced that it was Valentine's Day and the thought of it sunk me even further into depression. Until now I just knew that it was Friday and that Noah was going with Cindy to another doctor's appointment after the ultrasound. I wanted to follow up with Noah to see how everything went but I no longer had a right to know. Everything felt weird and different, and I had no one to talk to about it. Even though Mia was my best friend, I didn't feel right talking to her about Noah when he had been her best friend since they were little.

I patted Arlene's shoulder and smiled as I walked off to check on the rest of the tables, leaving her to enjoy the roses. I still had four hours left in my shift which felt like it was going to drag on forever until I got to go home and wallow in self-pity.

It was an hour until my shift was over when I heard the door chime and smiled when I looked up to see Chase, Mia, and Rylee come in. I nodded toward a booth in the back as I finished clearing the plates from a table that just left.

"Hey guys! What's my favorite little family doing here on Valentine's Day?" I smiled as I slid into the booth next to Mia, stealing Rylee as she sat her on the table in front of her.

"We thought it would be a nice treat to come for some peach cobbler," Mia said as she slid further into the booth, giving me more room to sit and play with the baby.

"We do have the best," I cooed as the baby looked up at me and smiled. "How many do you guys want?" I asked without looking at them.

"Just one is fine, we're sharing so it will be more romantic." Chase winked at Mia, her eyes rolling as he said it. I chuckled as I caught the interaction out of the corner of my eye.

"We definitely want two." She looked playfully at him before turning back to him. "He's crazy if he thinks he's getting a piece of my cobbler."

I glanced up to see Chase's expression change at the innocent innuendo his wife offered without noticing.

"Mmm baby, I've already had your cobbler but that doesn't stop me from wanting more." He wiggled his eyebrows suggestively at her as he leaned back and stretched his arm across the top of the booth.

"You're lucky you're cute." She playfully tossed an empty straw wrapper at him, hitting him in the forehead.

"I'm more than cute. I'm sexy."

"Alright, that's enough of the lovefest." I passed the baby back to Mia as I slid out of the booth and smoothed down my apron. "I'll go put in the order for two cobblers, you guys try to keep your hands to yourself while I'm gone."

I heard them laugh as I walked away, shaking my head. It was cute to see people flirting and in love but in my current situation, I wanted nothing to do with it. I glanced at the clock on the wall and saw that it was almost time for Cindy's appointment. Part of me wished that I could ask Chase and Mia about it to see how Noah was feeling about going to it but I knew that I couldn't. I needed to focus on getting through my shift then I could go home and work out until I burned off some of this anxiety and tension that seemed to linger around me.

Twenty
Noah

My foot tapped impatiently as I sat in the padded worn-out leather chair next to Cindy as we waited for the ultrasound tech to come in. I saw Cindy's eyes glare in my direction as she blew out an irritated breath.

"If you don't want to be here then you shouldn't have come." She turned her head to look at me.

"I didn't say I didn't want to be here. I'm here, aren't I?"

"Well, you could be a little more enthusiastic about it instead of sitting there tapping a hole into the ground with your foot."

I rolled my eyes and looked in the opposite direction as I continued tapping.

"Is there somewhere else you need to be instead?" She asked with an obvious jealously in her voice.

"Like I said, I'm here with you, aren't I? You don't need to worry about anything else." I leaned back against the seat and rested my hands on the cold metal armrests. Her mouth opened to say something else as the door opened and an older man with thinning gray hair walked into the room and looked at us. Her mouth closed and for once I was thankful for the interruption.

"Hello, I'm Doctor Edison. I'll be doing the ultrasound today since there have been some questions about the due date and size of the fetus." He extended a hand which I shook before leaning back into my seat.

I watched as he guided her on lifting her shirt before squirting the cold gel on her stomach. A few seconds later the baby appeared on the screen and I felt that same pull in my chest as the first time I saw it. He moved the wand around her stomach and stopped every few seconds to type something into the computer behind him. His brows pulled together as he pushed his bifocals back up his nose and leaned closer to the monitor, squinting at something.

I sat quietly, waiting for him to give us an update on the baby while Cindy looked more anxious than usual. Her hands were clenched tight around the metal bed frame as he removed the wand from her stomach and sat it in the holder next to the computer.

"Alright folks, it looks like the baby has grown some since the last ultrasound, which is great news."

"Perfect. Then everything is on track with my original due date," Cindy blurted out, talking over him before he could continue. His eyes narrowed at her as he shook his head and dismissed her.

"Not exactly. While the baby did grow, the baby is still measuring a full month behind."

"That's not possible, I know when I got pregnant. Maybe the baby is just naturally small?" Her tone was aggressive as she sat up straight in the bed and stared at the doctor.

"Some babies are smaller than others, but that's not what we're seeing here."

"Just give it to me straight doctor," I said as I made eye contact with him and ignored Cindy as she turned her glare to me. "What does it mean?"

"It means that there is a very healthy baby that is measuring on track for six months, not seven. I am very confident that the original conception date and due date are incorrect given the measurements and development of the baby that I saw today compared to the scan that was done two weeks ago."

"So that means," my voice trailed off as he gave me a knowing look.

"That means that this baby was not conceived in July. I would say it was conceived closer to the end of August or beginning of September."

I blew out a breath of relief as I ran a hand down my face, trying to process what all of this meant. I could feel the heat radiating from Cindy as she looked furiously at the doctor. I needed absolute confirmation that this baby wasn't mine but now was not the time to demand a paternity test from her unless I wanted to have some sort of medical device lodged up my ass.

"I know there's been some back and forth and discrepancies so I'm curious as to why this wasn't found on an earlier ultrasound?" I was playing the game the best way I knew how.

"I actually tried to pull copies of the original ultrasounds but we don't seem to have any in the system." He turned to look directly at Cindy. "Where were the other ones done? I can reach out to them to request copies of the original scan that was used to date the pregnancy."

The color drained from her face as her jaw dropped and for once, she was speechless.

"I um, I did them back home, before I moved here. I'll call and ask them for a copy."

"Just tell me the name of the clinic and I can request them since you're now under our care." He clicked his pen and held it over the paper on top of her chart, waiting for her to give him the information.

"I don't remember. I'll have to look for it when I get home," she replied through gritted teeth.

"Well, once we have those it will be easier to try to figure out what happened and why they would have given you a due date that doesn't match where the fetus is now in development." He shrugged and turned to face us on the swivel stool he was sitting on.

"Can you get a better idea based on her fundamental height?" I swallowed hard, praying that I remembered what Mia had told me about the measurements they could do that would confirm how far along she was. I watched as he stifled a laugh and turned to cough to cover it up.

"We can check the fundal height, but it's not 100% accurate either. It just gives us an idea of how big the uterus is and should more or less match to how many weeks pregnant a woman is."

I wanted to smack myself in the head for getting the name wrong and sounding like an idiot. I glanced at Cindy as she squirmed on the bed nervously. Something felt wrong and I needed to know what she was keeping from me. The doctor stood up and stood next to Cindy as he fumbled around in his pocket before pulling out a wound up tape measure and raising his eyebrows in question. She nodded and looked away as he felt around the top of her stomach with his fingers until he found what he was looking for and placed the end of the tape measure under his finger. I looked away to give her privacy as he pulled it lower and looked at the measurement.

"26 centimeters." He looked between us before turning around to write the information on the paper he had been using for the other notes.

I swallowed hard as my fists clenched. I turned to glare at her, panic on her face as she read my reaction. Tears started rolling down her face as she watched me get up and walk out of the room, slamming the door behind me.

Twenty One
Noah

I heard footsteps running behind me as I stalked off toward my truck, the snow starting to stick to the ground as it fell.

"Noah, wait!"

I gritted my teeth, my jaw tight, as I turned around and stared at Cindy. Her face was red and splotchy as she bent over to catch her breath from running after me.

"You have some fucking nerve." I shook my head at her, looking away to keep from saying anything more.

"Please, Noah, let me explain!" She reached for my arm, gasping when I jerked it away from her.

"Fine. Explain." I crossed my arms and leaned against the truck.

"It's complicated, I don't know why these doctors keep getting everything wrong. I swear, the doctors back home told me that I got pregnant in July, after I had been down here. These doctors must have outdated equipment or something?" Her voice rose an octave as her eyes danced wildly as she rambled on. "This baby is yours, Noah. I'm not that kind of girl who just sleeps around, you have to believe me." She put a hand on her stomach and rubbed it.

"Not that kind of girl? You were sucking my dick in the first five minutes after we met. You pulled me into the bathroom at the bar. You hiked up your skirt as you bent over and asked me to fuck you. So what kind of girl should I think you are?" I tilted my head and watched as her face turned red from embarrassment.

"I felt something with you Noah. And I know it's crazy to say you believe in love at first sight, but I do. I really, really do. You weren't just some random guy that I saw in the bar." She looked up at me with fresh tears in her eyes. "I knew you were the one, that's why I gave myself so freely to you."

I shook my head and pushed off the truck I had been leaning against when she startled rambling.

"I want a paternity test. Now. Before the baby is born." I looked at her sternly so she knew that I wasn't joking.

"That's crazy! This baby is yours Noah, we don't need a test to prove it."

"Everything in that appointment today says otherwise. You want me to go on believing that this baby is mine? Get the test."

"It would be stupid to do the test while I'm still pregnant. It could hurt the baby. Why would you want to hurt your baby?" Her eyes watched me cautiously as she wrapped her arms protectively around her waist.

"People get them all the time and the baby is fine. Either get the test on your own, or I'll get a court order. I want the results by next week." I glared at her as I swung my door open and climbed in, slamming it shut as she stared at me with her mouth open. I sped off, anger flowing through me as I headed off to deal with the next problem on my list.

The snow was coming down even harder by the time I pulled into the parking lot of Jade's apartment, a sure sign that this storm was going to be worse than they had predicted. I put the truck in park and made my way up the stairs, hoping she was actually home. I didn't see her car in the parking lot but that didn't mean she wasn't parked in the back lot.

I rang the doorbell and shoved my hands down into my pockets, shivering against the cold. A few minutes later I was getting ready to ring the doorbell again when the door opened and a shirtless man covered in tattoos opened the door. I blinked several times as I tried to figure out why a half-naked man was answering her door, let alone a guy I grew up with and couldn't stand.

"What's up, Noah?" He raised his arms above his head and held on to the door frame showing off a washboard stomach as he stretched.

"Is Jade here?" I asked annoyed.

He smugly looked over his shoulder toward the bedroom and turned back to look at me with the smug look still on his face.

"She's um, busy." He raised his eyebrows.

I was already feeling the anger from my encounter with Cindy so this was just adding fuel to the fire. I had known Chaz since elementary school and we spent most of our adolescence in chest matches over girls. For once, I wasn't in the mood to engage him.

"Fine, tell her I stopped by." I turned and walked off as I heard him chuckle before closing the door. This was not the romantic Valentine's Day I had planned.

THE CRADLE WILL FALL

Twenty Two
Jade

"Were you just talking to someone?" I asked Chaz as I walked into the living room, drying my hair with a towel. Work had been a rather slow day but I still couldn't wait to get home and wash the smell of greasy food off of me. The storm had hit early which left me thankful that I got home when I did. I glanced out the window and saw the snow coming down harder than it was before I jumped in the shower.

"Yeah, Noah came by looking for you." His tone was even as he watched for my reaction. My eyes darted up to his, my reaction apparent as he read the anger on my face.

"Sorry, you were in the shower. And... I kinda wanted him to feel a little jealous." He shrugged his shoulders as he walked to the fridge and pulled out a cold beer.

"That wasn't your call and I don't need you playing high school games, trying to make him jealous." I grabbed my cell phone off the kitchen counter and walked off to my room, closing the door behind me.

I wanted to talk to Noah, to see how things went with the appointment today but I felt so nervous about asking him. I didn't know where we stood, whether we were even friends still at this point. I held my phone in my hand, looking down at his name as my finger danced in circles, debating whether to push send or not. I climbed on my bed and curled up against a pillow as I chewed my nail while waiting for him to answer. What if he got the wrong idea when Chaz answered the door? Did he think I was already seeing someone else? Why had he shown up here unexpected anyways? The noise in my head grew louder as the ringing continued.

A few seconds later his voicemail picked up and I blew out the breath I had been holding. I sat my phone down beside me and shook my head in frustration for being so naive to think that he would actually want to talk to me after I broke up with him and then him finding a half-naked man in my apartment. I scooted down on the bed and stared up at the ceiling, contemplating my life decisions this week when I felt my phone vibrate against my butt. Excitement coursed through me when I picked it up and saw Noah's name.

"Hey," I practically whispered, smacking myself in the head for being so weird about it.

"Hey. I saw a missed call from you."

My stomach clenched as I heard how short he was with me, no warmth or flirting like usual.

"Yeah, Chaz told me you stopped by so I was calling to see what you had come by for."

Please say me... my brain pleaded as I waited, knowing full well that wasn't what he had come by for.

"Oh good, I'm glad your new boyfriend passed along the message."

I smirked when I heard the jealousy dripping through his voice.

"Yeah, he did. So what's up Noah? Why were you here?"

Now I could have played this the mature way and just been straight with Noah, letting him know that Chaz was far from being my boyfriend. He was only in my apartment because I quickly realized that I wasn't going to make nearly enough at SlowMo's to afford this apartment on my own. I had no choice but to find a roommate, and that roommate happened to be eating lunch at SlowMo's while I was working. I honestly didn't care who it was as long as they could come up with $400 by the first every month.

Part of me was still mad about everything that had happened this week and it actually felt good to hear Noah sounding jealous of another man given how jealous I had recently become of the girl he was having a baby with.

"I thought we could talk." He sighed and I could hear the phone shift against the stubble I pictured on his face.

"What did you want to talk about?"

"Does it even matter? We haven't been broken up a week and you already have another man answering your door half-naked Jade." There was a heavy mix of anger laced with jealousy and sarcasm in his voice that drove right to my core. Instantly I was seeing red.

"Really? You have the nerve to judge me for having another man in my apartment DAYS after we broke up when you had your dick in another woman HOURS after we broke up the first time?" My voice rose with my anger as I sat up and hung my legs over the side of the bed.

"Maybe this was a mistake," he bit out.

"Yeah, maybe it was." I slid my finger across the screen, hanging up before I tossed the phone down next to me as the fury raged through me. Who the hell did he think he was? The pot or the kettle? A few seconds later I felt my phone vibrate on the bed and without looking, I picked it up and answered.

"What?!" My chest rose and fell heavily as my feet tapped against the beige carpet beneath my feet.

"Woah. Did I catch you at a bad time?" Mia's voice came through the line making me regret not looking to see who was calling before I answered.

"I'm so sorry, Mia." I let out a heavy sigh and closed my eyes.

"Everything okay?"

"Yeah, I just got off the phone with Noah."

"So did he tell you?" Her voice trailed off quietly.

"Tell me what?" I didn't want to get into the details with Mia, to tell her that we were both acting so incredibly immature that we didn't get around to actually talking.

"The baby isn't his."

My heart dropped. I closed my eyes and brought my hand to my mouth as I forced myself to process what Mia had said.

"What? How does he know?"

"The ultrasound confirmed that the baby is still measuring around six months, not seven. Noah asked the doctor to check the measurement of her uterus and it agreed with the ultrasound. He said that Cindy started freaking out and begged him to believe her that the baby was his. He told her he wanted a paternity test."

"Oh my god. That's so crazy." My words were soft as I felt all of the anger I had felt minutes ago quickly disappear as I listened to Mia.

"Is she going to do the test?"

"He said that she said no, she didn't want to do it now and risk hurting the baby. But you know Noah, once his mind is set on something he doesn't give up. He's already been talking with a lawyer to get a court order for the test as soon as the baby is born."

"Will he have to do that?" I didn't know anything about family court or how to prove paternity but I knew that Noah was going to make sure he was fully prepared for whatever came his way.

"Honestly, I don't know. Everything is kind of in the air right now, we haven't heard anything from him since he called Chase earlier."

"Wow, I still can't believe it. So what's going to happen now with him and Cindy?"

"I don't know." She let out a heavy sigh at the same time I did. "Noah will probably do what Noah does best and continue to be the best dad he can be until it's been proven that it's not his baby. I don't think he could live with himself if he walked away and didn't do the right thing, and then some crazy bizarre turn of events happens and he finds out he actually is the dad. That would just kill him if he thought that even for one second, he didn't do his absolute best for his child."

I smiled knowing that what Mia had said was true. I leaned back against the pillow while we talked for a little bit, finally letting go of some of the anger and tension that had been building. The conversation had shifted to Rylee which was a nice distraction. Things felt easier when I had walked away from Noah knowing that he was having a baby with Cindy and needed to give the baby his full attention. But if what Mia said was true, that meant that things were different now. Noah might not be having a child at all. Cindy may not be a part of his life like she had planned. So what did this mean for us? Was there hope that we could actually be together without any obstacles getting in the way?

Twenty Three
Noah

I leaned back against the headboard and watched as the ring I bought for Jade spun in circles around my pinky, reminiscent of my life at the moment. How had things gone from good to absolute shit in less than a week? It was like someone took the threads that were holding everything together and unraveled them until there was nothing left.

My phone vibrated across the top of my nightstand, catching my eye as it slid around the wooden surface. I didn't have the energy to deal with whoever was calling this late and even if it was an emergency, there had to be someone more equipped than me to deal with it.

The ring continued to spin around my finger when my phone started to vibrate again. Annoyed I reached over and sat the ring on the nightstand as I picked up the phone. Either whoever was calling came to their senses and hung up before I could answer, or I had been so lost in thought that I hadn't paid attention to when it started ringing. Or maybe it was because it hadn't stopped ringing so there was no break for me to process. The screen showed eight missed calls, all back to back in the last two minutes.

I opened the missed call log and found Cindy's name listed for each call. It was after midnight which made me worry that something might be wrong with the baby. She didn't know anyone in town so it would make sense that I was the one she would call for help. I clicked on the last missed call and was getting ready to hit send to call her back when my phone started vibrating in my hand with another call from Cindy.

"What's up, Cindy. Is everything okay?" I climbed out of bed and stuffed my wallet back into my pocket in case I needed to leave.

"Everything's fine, why do you ask?" Her voice sounded strangely calm for someone who had been repeatedly calling me in the middle of the night until I picked up.

"Because you called like eight times. Back to back. In the middle of the night." I yawned as I sat back down on the bed, relieved that there was no need for me to go anywhere.

"I needed to talk to you, I don't like how we left things earlier."

"So you thought calling me nonstop this late was the way to get me to talk to you?"

"Well, I figured it was a good time since you were still up. And given the noise coming from Jade's apartment with her new roommate, I figured maybe you needed a friend to talk to."

"How did you know I was still up? And what noise are you talking about?" I felt my jaw set as I waited for her to confirm what I already knew. Jade was already sleeping with someone else.

"The lights were still on, silly." She laughed playfully before continuing like we were best friends. "You know, those kinds of noises. The noises that got us in the situation we're in."

I rolled my neck until I heard the familiar pop as I tried to get some relief from the mounting tension.

"I'm not in the mood to hear about Jade and honestly, I'm too tired to get into anything between us. So unless there's some sort of emergency, I'm gonna go and ask that you don't call me again. I'll reach out to you when I'm ready to talk." I paused as I waited for her to protest, surprised when she didn't. "And Cindy?"

"Yeah?" There was hope in her tone as I said her name.

"Stop driving by my house. People in this neighborhood don't take well to people who don't belong here. I wouldn't want anything bad to happen to you." I let the threat of my words linger in the air, a smug smile forming across my face as I heard the faint gasp on the other end before I hung up.

I felt an uneasiness as I sat my phone down, unsure of what I needed to do next. While sleep was the logical thing to do, I knew my mind was too busy to actually let it happen. I stripped off my clothes and took a hot shower, hoping the water would wash away everything that was wrong and give me the clean slate I needed. There wasn't much that I actually wanted to fix, and the only thing that I did want to fix was the one thing I had no control over.

I scrubbed my face and body vigorously as I focused on what I wanted, and more importantly, what I needed. Things with Cindy didn't need my attention right now. Whether she was lying about the baby being mine or not was irrelevant. I had already talked to the lawyer that my family had known since I was in diapers and he had walked me through the steps I would need to take to request the paternity test. Right now it was a waiting game, there was no reason to force her to get the test when there was a risk to the baby. Once the baby was born then I could request the paternity test through family court and go from there.

I had spent hours trying to process how I felt about the baby not being mine and part of me was fucking relieved that I wasn't having a baby with Cindy but the other part of me wasn't ready to fully accept it and cut ties with her yet. What if the reports were wrong and it really was my child? The thought of not being there from the very start for my own child gnawed away at me faster than a woodchuck with a fresh pile of wood.

Even if the baby was mine, that didn't mean that Cindy and I had to be together. I strongly believed that we could raise the child together and figure out how to co-parent. What I couldn't wrap my head around was Jade. I had tried talking to Mia about what happened with Jade after we left their house and everything fell apart but she didn't know what had happened either. She didn't divulge the details of what they had talked about, but she was just as surprised as I was when Jade called it off and broke up with me.

The water started to get cold as I turned the handle, feeling the cold air of the room surround me as soon as I stepped out of the shower. The storm had already been worse than they predicted and at this rate was expected to drop another twelve inches by the morning. While I was used to heavy snowstorms growing up in Colorado, we hadn't seen one this strong in almost a decade. I shivered as I quickly dried off and slid into the warmth of thick pajama pants before pulling a hoodie over my head.

I felt calmer after taking a thirty-minute shower even though my mind was no less chaotic than it was before. The only difference was now

I knew what I needed to do to win Jade back and I wasn't going to waste any time with sleeping.

The morning came faster than expected as I lost track of time working through every last detail of my master plan. My body felt heavy from the lack of sleep so I padded across the cold wood floor and started a pot of coffee, making sure to brew it stronger than usual. I walked back over to the couch and sat down, looking at the papers spread across the coffee table with the notes I had been making. My phone vibrated and I blew out a breath as I rolled my eyes and picked it, silently cursing that it better not be Cindy.

Jade: I think we need to talk. Can I come over?

Relief rushed over me as my fingers began moving quickly, asking her to give me thirty minutes before she came over. I was anxious to see her and find out what the fuck Chaz was doing in her apartment but I needed to hide what I was working on first.

The coffee had already finished brewing when I heard the doorbell ring, sitting an extra cup on the counter as I ran over to answer the door.

"Hey," I said as I opened the door and smiled, stepping to the side so she could come in and get out of the cold. She smiled back as she wiped her feet repeatedly on the welcome mat, getting rid of any excess snow that had stuck to her boots from outside. I watched as she pulled her gloves off before reaching up and pulling her beanie off, a wave of blonde hair falling down her back. It had only been a few days since I had seen her but I forgot just how breathtakingly beautiful she was.

There was a brown paper bag tucked up under her arm, a heavenly aroma filling the room which forced my stomach to grumble in response. I eyed the bag cautiously, knowing what was inside. She looked up and caught my eye, a smug smirk crossing her face as she tucked the bag tighter against her body as she turned away. She looked over her shoulder at me playfully as she walked in and sat on the couch, my eyebrow arched as I followed her.

"You better not be showing up to my house this early in the morning just to tease me with things I can't have," I warned.

She let out an exaggerated sigh as she fell back against the pillows on the couch and held the bag on her lap. There was the fun, flirty side of Jade that I had fallen in love with and had been missing ever since the stuff with Cindy started to interfere.

"I'll tell you what, you share some of your coffee, and I'll share some of my burrito." She patted the bag as she pulled her bottom lip between her teeth and slowly let it go.

"You can have the whole damn pot," I ran the pad of my thumb over her lip, freeing it from her teeth as I walked over to the counter, "Just stop biting your lip."

I heard a soft giggle behind me as I shook my head and poured two cups of coffee. When I turned around to walk back, Jade had sat the burritos on the coffee table and was staring at something in the middle of the table, a somber and serious look on her face.

"What's this?" She reached forward and picked up the engagement ring, holding it between her fingers as she studied me. I closed my eyes and shook my head, frustrated that I hadn't remembered to put the ring away with everything else.

"You weren't supposed to see that." I sat her cup on the coffee table in front of her and sunk down on the couch, taking a sip as I felt the scalding hot liquid burn its way down my throat. The pain was worth it to avoid having this conversation.

"You didn't answer my question." Her voice was quiet but her tone direct. She turned slightly to look at me, still holding the ring in the air.

I sat my cup down on the table in front of me and scrubbed a hand down my face, trying to think of how to tell Jade that I was planning to propose to her before she broke up with me. Everything had changed and shifted which left me feeling uncertain of whether it was even worth talking about right now. There were so many other things we still needed to discuss. Things like Chaz. In her apartment.

"It's a ring." I turned and looked her in the eye, challenging her. She licked her lips the way she does every time she gets nervous, much to my satisfaction. At least I wasn't the only one squirming in my seat.

"I can see that. Why do you have an engagement ring?"

"Because Jade, I was planning to ask you to marry me. To start a life with me. To show you that no matter what was happening with Cindy and the baby, you still came first." I looked away when I saw her flinch from the change in my tone.

She stayed quiet as she looked at the ring and sighed, leaning forward to sit it down on the table where she had found it.

"I'm sorry Noah, maybe I shouldn't have come here." She ran the palms of her hands down her jeans and stood up.

"You came here for a reason, Jade, let's just talk and get everything out in the open. If you still don't want to be with me, that's fine, but I at least deserve to know what the fuck actually happened."

"I told you what happened Noah, I told you that I was leaving so you could be with your child. It wasn't that I had stopped loving you. I loved you so much that I was willing to walk away from you so you could be the father you wanted to be without having someone complicate it for you, you selfish prick." She plopped back down on the couch and glared at me before picking up her burrito from the table and nodding at mine. "Eat your damn burrito before it gets cold."

I let out a chuckle, thankful that she hadn't decided to walk away, again. We ate in silence while taking sips of coffee to wash it all down until there was nothing left to fill the awkward silence between us once we were finished. She leaned back against the couch and closed her eyes.

"Why was Chaz in your apartment?"

I watched as her lips pursed in a thin line as she thought about how to answer me. I braced myself for the blow that was coming as my fists clenched at my sides.

"He's my new roommate." She turned to look at me, studying my face as confusion spread across it.

"He's what?"

"My roommate."

"Why do you need a roommate?"

"I took quite a pay cut from what I was making at the bank, I didn't have a choice."

I leaned forward, resting my elbows on my knees, and looked at her.

"You could have come to me, I would have found a way to help you."

"Seriously? You're going to help me with paying my rent each month after we break up? You're a good guy, Noah, but no one is that nice."

"Try me."

"It's just ridiculous to even think that! You have your own bills to pay and possibly a baby on the way, you can't possibly afford to pay $400 a month towards rent for someone that you're not even dating."

"Jade, I would pay your whole fucking rent if it meant you didn't have him as your roommate," I gritted through my teeth, the tension in my body coming back.

"Why? What's your problem with him?"

"I don't trust him, Jade, and I don't think you should either."

"Are you that jealous?" She raised her eyebrows as if this was the most insane thing she had ever heard.

"Abso-fucking-lutely I'm jealous, why wouldn't I be?" I studied her as she took in my words. "But aside from that, I wouldn't trust him with anyone. Not just because it's you. Did you even question him or interview him before you asked him to move in with you?" My heart was pounding in my ears the more my anger escalated at the thought of Chaz living with her. Her chest fell and I watched as she looked away and chewed on her fingernail.

"Jade, did you find out anything about him before he moved in with you? Or did you just take the first person that responded to your ad?"

"I um, I didn't run an ad." She slowly looked at me, still chewing her fingernail.

"So you just approached a random stranger and asked him to live with you?" I could hear the stern tone in my voice as her eyes looked panicked.

"I didn't go seeking anyone out, Noah. It wasn't like that. He was eating lunch, I was his waitress, he was complaining about needing to find a new place to live and I muttered something about needing to find a roommate then we just started talking and found a solution to our problems." She gave me a pointed look.

"Whose idea was it for him to move in?"

I watched as she looked away, avoiding eye contact with me.

"Jade..."

She blew out a long, steady breath before turning her attention back to me.

"His."

I dropped my head into my hands and shook my head.

"What's the big deal, Noah? What has he done that's so bad that I should know about?"

"He's not a good person Jade, I grew up watching him manipulate people and take advantage of women the moment his family moved here from Eastern Point. And honestly, nothing good comes from that town. His family has swindled people out of money, forced their way into partnerships that should never have been formed, and everything they do is shady."

"Okay, I get it. I shouldn't have let him move in with me, I should have asked around about him before making a decision. But what am I supposed to do now? He's already paid this month's rent and I really need that money."

"The offer to move in with me is still on the table."

"You're relentless." She shook her head as she struggled to keep the smile off of her face when she saw mine.

"Yeah, but deep down you still think I'm adorable."

"Maybe." Her lips twisted up into a smile as I reached over and rested my hand next to hers.

"Maybe is all I need," I growled as I pulled her over to me, enjoying the sound of her giggle as I tickled her sides. There was still a lot we needed to work out but for now, I wanted to just live in the moment, and that moment was filled with beautiful laughter.

Twenty Four
Jade

I had spent Saturday morning at Noah's, trying to work things out between us but when I left that afternoon I still felt like I didn't know where we stood with each other. We were friendly yet flirty. Friends but not lovers. Definitely not enemies. There didn't seem to be a clear definition of what we were and I hated it. I wanted to be able to move forward but I didn't know which direction I was supposed to go.

The evening was quiet, Chaz was already gone when I had gotten back from Noah's earlier. There was nothing from him to indicate when he was planning to be back, and I felt stupid for feeling like I needed him to check in with me. He was a roommate, not a prisoner.

I was relieved to have some time to myself in the apartment but Noah's warning about Chaz kept ringing through my head, forcing me to doubt whether I made a good choice with letting him move in. Either way, it was too late now, I had already agreed to it and he had moved in. I could technically ask him to leave, give him a month to find a new place, but I also desperately needed his half of the rent.

The storm outside had finally started to calm after it dumped another six inches of snow on the few feet that had been accumulating since yesterday afternoon. Mia and I were supposed to have dinner together but that had been canceled so neither of us would have to go out in the cold. I felt restless as I paced the kitchen, debating on whether to cook or order food in. While cooking would distract me more, I worried I would be too distracted and end up burning it. I gave up, ordered a pizza, and poured a glass of wine while I watched the light snow as it fell outside while I waited.

Forty minutes later my doorbell rang, the savory aroma of pizza filling my apartment as I opened the door. I tipped the kid double since he had to come out in the bad weather to deliver and sat the pizza on the counter after he left. I took a deep breath as I opened the lid, my mouth watering in anticipation. I reached in, pulled out a slice and took a bite, lifting the trail of cheese that had fallen against my chin into my mouth when I heard the doorbell again.

I sat down the slice and wiped my face with a napkin as I walked over to the door, expecting it to be the delivery guy who had forgotten something. My stomach dropped when Cindy greeted me from the other side, I wasn't in the mood to deal with her tonight.

"Hey, Cindy. What's up?"

"I really hate to ask, but I was wondering if you could help me move something I'm trying to get the nursery set up before the baby gets here, but I can't lift anything heavy and I really don't know who else to ask since Noah isn't talking to me."

I saw the look in her eyes when she mentioned his name, the sadness that lingered when she acknowledged that he wasn't talking to her. I didn't want to help her but deep down inside I knew that it was the right thing to do. Aside from the handful of reasons that I didn't like her, I wasn't the type of person that would deny someone help when they needed it.

"Sure. Let me grab my phone and keys, then I'll be right there."

"It shouldn't take more than a second," her voice pleaded with mine and I felt thankful that she didn't seem to want me in her apartment any longer than I wanted to be there.

"Okay," I sighed, "Let's go."

I closed the door to my apartment behind me as I followed her outside and into her apartment. I had only seen inside for a brief second when she first moved in but now that I was inside and looking around, a feeling of dread rushed over me as I took in the room around me and heard the click as the door shut behind us. I wanted to turn around and look at Cindy, to see where she was, but my eyes were glued to the wall that we shared where picture frames were hung neatly around a black metal Family sign. The sound of the lock clicking into place followed by the slide of the deadbolt forced my attention away from the photos and over to Cindy.

"Do you like them?" she asked as she walked over and stood next to me, rubbing her stomach as she admired the collage on the wall. Each frame had a picture of Noah and I in it, however all of my pictures had been replaced with pictures of Cindy. The majority of the pictures were from Chase and Mia's wedding, however, a few were recent and I recognized them immediately. Noah and I at Liam's birthday party. Noah and I at Chase and Mia's for dinner. Noah holding Rylee. Noah at work.

"They're nice…" My voice trailed off as I struggled with what to say.

"I wanted to make sure that the baby had plenty of pictures on the wall to look at as they grow up, so they can see how happy mommy and daddy have always been." Her smile spread clear across her face as she beamed at the wall. I licked my lips nervously and tucked a stray piece of hair back behind my ear. I wanted desperately to get out of there.

"So, what did you need help moving?" I turned to face her, hoping to bring her back to the task at hand so I could be done and get back to the comfort of my own apartment while I tried to forget this was on the other side.

"I would say your body, but that would just sound crazy!" She let out a hysterical laugh as she threw her head back and snorted. I watched, my eyes wide with horror, as she continued.

"Well, if you don't need my help then I guess I can just let myself out." I forced a smile and kept my voice light, trying not to draw any attention to myself as I slowly started walking to the door.

"Yeah, I'm afraid it's not that easy, Jade." Her laughter stopped as she gave me a pointed look.

"What's not?"

"You leaving. I simply can't let you do that."

"Why not?"

"Because, if I let you go, you'll just keep getting in the way." She stepped closer to me. "And I'm sick and tired of you being in my way."

"Cindy, I'm not trying to be in your way. I just want to leave and go back to my apartment. I have no reason to stay here when it obviously upsets you so much." I tried to take another step towards the door, forcing my brain to flip the order of the apartment so I could guide myself to maneuver backward as I kept her focused on my words.

"You don't get it. As long as you're around, Noah isn't going to stop chasing you. And if he's always chasing you, then he's not going to be around for me and this baby."

"Noah and I broke up, Cindy. I'm not keeping him from you."

She watched me through narrowed eyes as I took the tiniest of steps backward, trying to get to the door without drawing too much attention.

"Then why were you at his house this morning?" she spat out angrily.

How did she know I was at his house? Had she been watching me? Or had she been watching both of us?

"I went by to give him back the key to his house that he had given me."

"The key that SHOULD HAVE BEEN MINE." She took a few steps closer, closing the distance between us faster than I had anticipated which meant the window I had for getting out the door without her catching me was getting narrower by the second.

"Do you get it now, Jade? He's willing to give you everything you want, and yet you still don't want to be with him. You don't love him. You don't want to be with him. But I do, and I can't because as long as you're around he will continue to keep trying to win you over. So now I'm stuck making sure that never happens."

"What exactly do you plan to do?" I rolled my eyes for even asking the question, but she had already closed the space between us, and I was out of ideas for how to get out without causing a commotion. She was close enough that I could smell the garlic on her breath from the container of takeout on the counter behind her. Any possible escape options would now have to be heavily weighed given that she was pregnant, and I had no desire to hurt a pregnant woman or unborn child.

"I haven't decided what your ultimate fate will be just yet, but you won't be going anywhere any time soon. For now, it will look like you just up and left. And once Noah is over it, and we start building our life together, I'll figure out what to do with you."

"So you're going to lock me in your apartment until Noah falls in love with you?" I arched an eyebrow, getting a look of anger immediately in response from her.

"Exactly."

I rolled my eyes and turned, reaching for the doorknob. Whatever she thought she had planned wasn't my problem anymore. I had no desire to hurt a pregnant woman so I sincerely hoped she wouldn't force me to do so.

"Yeah, I'm leaving. Good luck with everything, Cindy," I said smugly as I felt the knob turn in my hand seconds before I felt the impact of something heavy making contact with the back of my head, forcing me to the ground.

Twenty Five
Noah

I was feeling more and more anxious as the hours went by and I still hadn't heard from Jade. We had agreed to get together Sunday morning for brunch but after she hadn't responded to my first text this evening, I started to worry that she might stand me up. Things weren't necessarily back to normal between us yet, but I had felt like we were on the right path when she left earlier today. It was almost nine o'clock and I had been texting her for over three hours with no response. I was starting to get worried. It wasn't like her to completely ignore me, even if she was mad at me.

I picked up my phone and called Mia, remembering that they were supposed to have dinner together tonight when Chase asked if I wanted to have a guys night while the girls gossiped. Last I knew it had been canceled, but maybe I was wrong and she wasn't answering because she was at Mia's. After the fifth ring, I was getting ready to hang up when I heard her answer.

"Hey Mia, I'm sorry it's late. Is Jade there with you?" I tried to keep the panic out of my voice while also not sounding like a completely whipped pussy.

"No, we decided to do dinner another night. Why? What's wrong?" Her voice was filled with concern which meant she had already picked up on mine.

"I haven't heard from her in a few hours and I'm starting to get worried."

"Have you been calling her?"

"No, just texting. I called once but it went to voicemail."

"Did you make her mad?"

I chuckled as I clearly saw Mia's face with her arched eyebrow as she asked the question, knowing that was a good likelihood. I sighed heavily and ran a hand through my hair as I asked myself the same question.

"I don't think so? If I did, I have no idea what I did this time."

"I know things have been off between you guys, maybe she just needs some space," Mia spoke softly, the way she always did when she didn't want to hurt my feelings.

"Maybe. But she seemed fine when she was here earlier."

"She was there? At your house?"

I let out a laugh at her reaction.

"Yeah, why is that so hard to believe?"

"It's not, sorry. I just didn't know she was planning to go over there. When we talked on the phone last night she was pretty fired up about your guys' phone call."

"She actually surprised me when she asked to come over this morning. But by the time she left, we were laughing and joking just like we used to. She even agreed to have a late breakfast with me tomorrow."

"Brunch, Noah, the word is brunch." She giggled, knowing how much I hated the word.

"Fine, we were supposed to have BRUNCH and shit tomorrow," I joked.

"Does that make it feel manlier to you?"

"Fuck yeah it does."

We both laughed for a few seconds before turning our attention back to the reason that I had called.

"So what should I do? Do you think I should go to her apartment to check on her?"

"Honestly, I wouldn't. I know Jade and if she's purposely not answering you, she won't be happy about you showing up unexpected."

I could hear as she covered the phone, talking in the background.

"I'll go check on her and update you after I've talked to her."

"Absolutely not, Mia. I'm not having you go out in this weather, this late at night."

"You don't have a choice. I'm a big girl Noah, and believe it or not, I actually know how to drive both at night and in bad weather. I did live in Boston you know?"

"Chase is going to fucking kill me..."

"You're right about that." I could hear him in the background and rolled my eyes, hating the thought that Mia had to do this because of me.

"Can I at least meet you at your house and drive you over? That way I know that you're safe?"

"I'll be fine. Just stay where you are and keep your phone handy. I'll send an update when I have one."

"Thanks, Mia."

I heard the click as the call disconnected and held my phone against the bridge of my nose as I closed my eyes and prayed that everything was fine and that I didn't just send my best friend's wife out in bad weather at night for some stupid reason, like Jade's phone died. I sat on the edge of the couch and waited impatiently for an update.

Twenty Six
Jade

My eyes fluttered open as I tried to move my arms, feeling them bound behind my back. I looked around the room, recognizing the setup of Cindy's apartment as I heard footsteps in the back bedroom. Music was playing faintly in the background as she sang along. My head was killing me, whatever she had used to knock me out had left a terrible headache behind. I tried moving my legs and felt the tightness of the rope around them, pinning me in place to the wooden chair that I was sitting on.

I blew out a heavy breath through my nose, my mouth gagged by the bandana that was tied behind my head. Apparently, she wasn't joking about me not leaving this apartment. I tried again to wiggle myself free as the rope refused to give. My body sagged in response as I saved my energy and stopped trying for the moment. I needed to be smart about this if I wanted to escape, and I needed to give Cindy more credit than I had since I never would have imagined she would be capable of pulling this off. In hindsight, I should have trusted my instincts earlier and left the second things didn't feel right. Hell, I should have said no to begin with. Being a nice person wasn't always what it was cracked up to be.

The sound of the music in the bedroom started to get louder as I heard her footsteps approach. She walked into the kitchen and her eyes lit up when she saw that I was awake, her fingers working to turn the music down on her phone.

"Oh good, you're awake," she cooed as she walked over and watched me like I was some sort of caged animal that might bite if she got too close.

I watched her every movement as she walked behind me and untied the bandana, not taking it out of my mouth, just untying it from the back.

"Can you be a good girl and not scream?"

I nodded my head yes slowly, desperate for her to get it out of my mouth.

"You sure? Because these walls are pretty thin and I know for sure that you're a screamer." She leaned forward and wiggled her eyebrows suggestively at me. I forced a deep breath in through my nose, trying to force myself not to throw up on her. A few seconds later she slowly pulled the bandana away. Even if I wanted to scream, no one would hear it. Her apartment was the very last apartment at the end of the building and unless Chaz had made it home, no one would hear unless they were inside my apartment.

I took a few deep breaths after the bandana was gone and studied her as she pulled another wooden chair out from behind the table and slid it in front of me, sitting down to face me. As she sat in front of me I noticed a necklace around her neck and looked down to see the locket my sister had given me. The locket that I had cried over for weeks after it went missing. Looking back at the day I found her snooping through my desk, I should have known that she had taken it when I couldn't find it. The anger raged inside of me as I stared at it, something that was so sacred and special to me, now tainted by her touch.

"Let me go, Cindy," I warned as I stared into her icy cold eyes. "Now."

"Aww, that's cute," she mocked me as she faked a smile. "You really think that you can just get whatever you want, don't you?"

I ignored her question as I looked past her, not giving her the satisfaction of making eye contact as she searched my face.

"What is it that big, bad, Jade wants? Huh? Because it sure as hell isn't the man who is bending over backward to give you the world. You are so selfish and entitled, you don't even realize what a good thing you have." She shook her head and looked at me. "Sorry, had."

"I guess I should be asking you the same question. What is it that Cindy so desperately wants and can't have? Besides the love of a man that will never be hers." I pursed my lips as I glared at her, my anger starting to rise.

"You have NO idea what you're talking about. Once you're out of the way and he sees how hard you were to please, he'll be desperate for someone like me to love him. To show him how good it can be without having to constantly work to try to make someone happy who doesn't even know what happiness is."

"And you know what happiness is? You've had a love that was so grand, it taught you how to be exactly what he wants and needs?" My voice was laced thick with sarcasm as I watched the color drain from her face.

"I know that he deserves a hell of a lot better than you."

"Yeah, I could say the same." I arched my brow and tilted my head. I may be bound to a chair but that didn't mean that I didn't know how to deal with jealous, insecure girls like her. I had been doing it my entire life and was raised by one.

"You'll learn to respect me and to watch what you say around me." Cindy stood up and slammed her chair down beside me, forcing me to flinch from the sound. I watched as she walked off down the hallway and slammed the bedroom door shut behind her. I closed my eyes and leaned my head back as I tried to figure out how to get myself out of this mess.

THE CRADLE WILL FALL

Twenty Seven
Noah

"Mia, is she alright?" I didn't bother with saying hi as I rushed to answer my phone when I saw it light up with Mia's name.

"She wasn't home."

"Are you sure?" I knew it sounded stupid but I had no idea where Jade could be if she wasn't at home, and sure as hell wasn't at my place.

"Yeah, I rang the doorbell 3 or 4 times and waited, there was no answer."

"That's strange."

"I'm sure it's nothing. Maybe she went to bed early and just didn't hear it. Or maybe she went to the store. You know Jade, she's never one to stay still for too long." There was hope in Mia's voice that I found myself clinging to.

"Yeah, maybe." I got up and paced the small distance between the living room and kitchen as I tried to figure out where she could be.

"Noah, give it up for tonight. I'm sure she's fine. I'll try to call her in the morning and I'll let you know once I talk to her. Get some sleep."

"Yes, mother," I teased with a smile before hanging up.

It was driving me crazy that I hadn't heard from Jade all night and I tried not to let the nagging feeling that something was wrong get under my skin. I walked to the fridge and pulled out a cold beer, thankful that there was still one left given that I hadn't been to the grocery store since before the storm hit. Something else to add to my to-do list in the morning before I set up brunch for Jade.

I had planned everything out and spent the day going over all of the details for tomorrow after Jade left. The meal was planned out and a grocery list made with the items I would need. While I technically should be sleeping given that I was exhausted from not sleeping last night, my mind couldn't stop thinking about whether she would say yes tomorrow when I officially asked her to marry me. She had already seen the ring so the surprise of it was out of the way, though I didn't know whether that actually worked in my favor or not. She didn't give away much of a reaction but I could swear that for a split second, I saw her eyes light up. If the circumstances were different, I could imagine that she would have been excited to have me propose and there would have been no doubt that her answer would be yes.

I leaned back against the couch and took a long swig of my beer as I felt my phone vibrate next to me. I reached down, my fingers trembling with excitement that it was Jade and Mia was right about her being busy or asleep. As I unlocked the screen my face fell when I found a text message from Cindy instead.

Cindy: I'm really sorry. I don't know how to get you to talk to me but I really think that if you would just hear me out, everything would be okay.

I slid my finger over the button to erase the message and sat my phone down. No matter what was happening between Jade and I, there was nothing left for me to say to Cindy. I was a master at reading people and the way she reacted at the doctor's office with the ultrasound confirmed that she had been lying and that the baby wasn't mine. All that was left to do at this point was to wait for the baby to be born so we could do a paternity test to confirm.

Twenty Eight

Jade

The light trickled into the room as I slowly rolled my head forward, the pain from it hanging down while I slept was excruciating. Add to it the pain of getting whacked in the back of the head by some heavy object and the headache was unbearable. I looked around the room, trying to find Cindy, hoping she had left and I would have time to try to figure out how to get myself out of this mess.

It was Sunday morning so the likelihood of her going anywhere was slim. She didn't have work and if she set foot inside of a church I was pretty sure it would immediately burst into flames. Suddenly I found myself picturing it and shook my head to clear the terrible thoughts as they forced their way further into my mind. Heavy footsteps padded down the hallway and I let out a soft sigh knowing that she was still there and not about to burn in hell like she deserved.

I tried finding a clock to check the time, remembering that I was supposed to meet Noah at his house for brunch at eleven. Anxiety started to build as I thought about how he would feel if he thought that I had stood him up after we had talked yesterday and he had hinted at having a very special surprise for me at brunch today. I chewed the inside of my lip to keep the tears from my eyes as my heart silently broke at the thought of the pain it would cause him when I didn't show up.

Maybe if anything, Cindy would have come to her senses this morning and would decide to let me go. They say pregnancy makes some women do crazy things, maybe that included holding people hostage in your apartment while confessing your undying love for their boyfriend.

I watched as Cindy walked into the kitchen, a red flannel robe loose over her flannel pajamas that barely covered her stomach as it forced the top up and left a sliver exposed. Her hair was piled high into a messy bun on top of her head and she had bags under her eyes as if she hadn't slept well. That would make two of us. She kept her focus on digging through the refrigerator as she pulled things out and sat them on the counter between the fridge and the stove. Next, she reached for the cast iron skillet that was sitting on the counter and glanced at me before sitting it on the stove and turning the gas on. The look that she gave me forced me to wonder if that's what she had used to knock me out. It made sense given that it was sitting on the counter, close to where she had been standing last night.

She poured oil into the pan and shook it back and forth, forcing the liquid to coat the inside. I watched as she aggressively opened the carton of eggs and banged each one on the side of the counter before dropping the raw egg into the skillet. A few minutes later she tossed in a handful of cut veggies from a Tupperware container she had pulled out from the fridge and added a handful of shredded cheese to the top.

"We're having omelets for breakfast," she said angrily as she looked over her shoulder at me.

"None for me, thank you." I kept my voice soft so as to not anger her further.

Too late. Her head whipped around as she glared at me.

"You're too good for the breakfast I'm making for you?"

"No, not at all. I'm allergic to eggs." I offered a tight smile that didn't reach my eyes. She studied me as she held the spatula in the air, one hand on her hip as she thought about what I said.

"What happens when you eat them?"

"I... can't breathe." I was reluctant to tell her for fear that she would use this information to actually try to kill me, but I also risked her getting so offended that I didn't eat them, that she still forced me to eat them and indeed, killed me.

"Interesting," she whispered as she pulled her bottom lip between her teeth before turning back to the skillet and flipping the omelet.

I sat in silence as I watched her finish cooking her eggs before sitting down across from me to eat them. My stomach grumbled in response to the smell, remembering that I hadn't actually eaten dinner last night. I could feel as my arms started to go numb, my body desperate to be free of this position. Just to stretch for a quick second and regain some of the blood flow would be heavenly.

Cindy got up and walked to the sink, sitting her plate and fork down before turning around and looking at me. There was a look of excitement on her face and I had no idea what she was thinking but deep down I knew that it wasn't going to be good.

"I'm going to go shower, then we'll get started. We have a lot to get done today." She smiled as she turned and walked down the hallway to the bathroom, the sound of water running a few seconds later.

I desperately tried pulling at the rope again, using everything I had in me to try to force it to give. Even just a small amount, I could try to make it work. There had to be a way to get out of this rope. After a few minutes of struggling, I was out of breath and my muscles were burning. I leaned against the wooden back of the chair and let out a frustrated growl. Never in my life had I ever felt so physically helpless. I looked around the room and studied everything, looking for anything that I could use to try to cut the rope with.

Aside from the collage of photos on the wall, there wasn't much else in the apartment in way of decorations. The apartment had come fully furnished, just like mine had, however it didn't look like Cindy had bothered with adding any additional decorations since she had moved in. Off in the corner of the kitchen was a knife block that was tucked too far back for me to try to reach without getting caught. I definitely wouldn't be able to grab it with my hands given that they were bound behind a chair and the space on the counter was small with the cabinets hanging above. If I had more time I could try to nudge it free with my head and see if I could knock the block over, remove one or two with my teeth, and then turn around and grab it with my hand, slicing it perfectly through the rope and freeing myself.

Oh, who the fuck was I kidding? This wasn't some cheesy Hollywood action flick with unbelievable stunts that lead the good guy to defying all odds and miraculously escaping the bad guy. This was real life and there was literally a negative 1% chance of that plan actually working. I shook my head in irritation as Cindy walked back into the room, her wet hair wrapped in a towel on her head.

"What's the matter?" she asked curiously as she watched my discomfort as I tried to adjust myself in the chair.

"Nothing, I'm just uncomfortable from not being able to move."

"Oh, well that's not a problem. I plan to untie you in just a few minutes so we can get on with our day and get the stuff done that we need to." She smiled as she pulled her hair down from the towel and quickly rubbed the towel over her hair before combing it.

I was confused as to what she thought we had planned for the day but relieved that it would include her untying me. Once I was free I could fight my way out of here and be done with this bullshit.

"What exactly are we doing today?" I asked as I continued to move my hands behind me, thankful for the movement as they started to go numb again.

"Well, first, you're going to text Noah and break things off with him. For good." She gave me a look equivalent to that of a teacher catching students passing notes in class.

"I can't do that."

"Doesn't matter. I'll do it then. Either way, you're breaking up with him."

"I mean, I can't do that because I don't have my phone. Remember yesterday when you convinced me that I didn't need it because we would be quick? I don't think Noah is going to buy it if I break up with him from your phone."

"Well then, we'll just have to go get your phone, won't we?"

"Just untie me and I'll go grab it." My voice rose a tiny bit, giving away the hope that had started to bloom inside.

"Yeah, sure. Like I'm that stupid." She rolled her eyes and sat down the comb she had been using on her hair. "I'll go next door and get it."

"The door is locked."

"So then I'll knock and ask Chaz to get it for me."

"He won't. He doesn't know you."

"Trust me, I have my ways." She jerked her head, forcing her wet hair over her shoulder as she walked past me and opened the door. I waited to hear the click as it shut and was surprised when I noticed that it was still open a sliver and she hadn't noticed. I pushed myself as far to the side as I could without falling over as I struggled to hear what was happening outside. I could hear the faint footsteps through the wall and knew that Chaz was home. A few seconds later the door opened.

"Can I help you?" His deep voice vibrated through the walls.

"Hi, I'm Cindy, I live next door." She paused and I watched as she pulled the door shut the rest of the way when she must have seen that it wasn't closed all the way.

"Anyways, Jade is helping me build some furniture for the baby's nursery and she accidentally left her phone inside and asked if I could come grab it for her."

"Okay, go ahead and come on in. I think I saw it next to the pizza she left out on the counter last night. Is she okay?" There was a protective concern in his voice and hope filled me that he would act on his instincts and demand to come to Cindy's apartment to check on me. But then again I didn't know the guy and if what Noah said about him was true, I couldn't imagine that he had that much empathy in him to actually give a damn.

"Yeah, she actually stayed the night with her boyfriend last night. I heard them fighting earlier in the evening then there was some pretty loud making up before they went back to his place, if you know what I mean."

I could hear her giggling as my blood pressure started to rise.

"Here's her phone. Did you need anything else?" Chaz asked, completely dismissing her comment about Noah and I.

"I think that's it. I'm sure I'll be back if there's something else."

"Yeah, sure. Or maybe Jade can just come get her stuff herself."

I could hear the tension in his voice and knew that if I didn't act now, I would miss an opportunity. I didn't peg him as being the kind of guy who would ever hurt a woman, but at this point, I needed a man with huge muscles to come in and save the day, as lame and sexist as that sounded. I could hear their footsteps as they walked back to the door and knew the window was quickly closing. Without giving it another thought, I started screaming as loud as I could, which was rather hard given how dry my mouth was.

I was still screaming when I saw the door fly open, Cindy's eyes wide with anger as she slammed the door shut and stormed over to me.

Within seconds I felt the impact from her fist crashing into the side of my face, forcing my head to whip to the side in response.

"What the fuck do you think you're doing?" she growled, keeping her voice low enough for me to hear as she towered over me and glared at me.

The pain spread across my cheek and up toward my eye as I slowly turned around and gave her the dirtiest look I could muster.

"You do that again and I will make your life even more of a living hell," she warned as she looked me up and down and walked past me, sitting my phone on the table. "I'll give you a few minutes to calm down before I untie you. I wouldn't want anything unfortunate to happen to you."

Twenty Nine
Noah

It was afternoon when I looked down at my phone again, disappointed that there were no texts or missed calls from Jade. The champagne sat in a bucket of melted water while the food was cold and looked like it had seen better days. The same song had played for the tenth time as the romantic playlist of her favorite songs looped back around. And the most depressing thing to fill the room was the thought that I had finally won her heart and thought that today would be the day that I finally asked her to marry me.

A text message came through from Chase, asking when they could come by to congratulate the happy couple. I shot him a quick text telling him that happy endings only exist in fairytales which meant it wasn't possible for me given that I was living in a nightmare. He offered to come by and hang out if I wanted to talk but it didn't feel like there was anything that was going to change my mood so I told him not to bother.

An hour later I was finishing up cleaning the kitchen and throwing out the spoiled food when my phone vibrated with a new text message. I sat the trash bag down next to the island as I picked up my phone and saw Jade's name. A tingle of excitement washed over me as I took a deep breath before opening it.

Jade: Things are over between us. Please don't try to talk me out of this decision, we both know it's best if we go our separate ways. You need to be there for Cindy and the baby. I'll be leaving town to make this a cleaner break from each other.

My stomach clenched as I read the words over and over, hoping that something might change each time I read them. That I might have read it wrong the first time and instead of breaking my heart, she was actually confessing her love for me. That I wasn't the only one who felt like they were drowning in a sea of misery.

I exited the message and slammed the phone down on the island as I stormed off to my weight room. I had too much pent up frustration and steam that I needed to burn off the only way that I knew how. Well, the only way that wouldn't get me into another Cindy situation.

Thirty
Jade

The day felt like it had dragged on forever as Cindy paced back and forth around the room, staring at her cell phone in her hand as she muttered under her breath about why Noah hadn't texted her back. My stomach had been sour ever since she had shown me the text message she had sent to him from my phone, confirming that I never wanted to see him again. My heart ached when I thought of what Noah must be feeling right now, especially after I had seen the engagement ring at his house yesterday.

Things with Noah had changed drastically over the last few months and a huge part of me was desperate to see where things could go with us. Part of me questioned whether we would be moving along at the same pace in our relationship if everything with Cindy had never happened. If he wasn't being forced into having a baby with another woman, would he still be interested in settling down? I saw the way he beamed when he held Rylee and the way his eyes lit up when he talked about the cute little things she did when he was with her so that made me think that maybe Rylee was also responsible for the change in him.

My arms were starting to ache even more and my butt was killing me from sitting in the same position for so long. I was desperate to be able to move, to sit in any other position than this one.

"Cindy, do you think I can get up to use the restroom?" I tried to keep any hint of anger out of my voice as I prayed that she had at least one tiny human bone in her evil pregnant body. She looked over at me, barely taking her eyes off of her phone, while she thought about what I was asking.

"Seriously, unless you want me to pee on your chair, I need you to untie me and let me use the restroom." I watched as she looked back toward the bathroom, still doubting whether she should let me go. "Cindy, we live in the same apartment. You know as well as I do that there's no way for me to escape from the bathroom. There's a tiny little window in there that even a child wouldn't fit through. I just need to use the bathroom, and I would love to stretch my legs for a minute."

"Fine. But I'm making sure that you're not going to try anything." She walked past me and sat her cell phone down on the kitchen counter behind me and opened a drawer before slamming it shut. A few seconds later I felt the rope loosen around my feet then the rope around my hands fell to the floor. I wanted to reach forward and stretch, to allow my body to get the blood flowing back to where it had been cut off, but the sound of her cocking a gun behind my head kept me completely still.

"Get up and walk slowly to the bathroom," she instructed.

I glanced out of the corner of my eye as I started walking toward the bathroom and saw her holding a small black handgun pointed at my head as she walked behind me. Any plan I had for trying to overpower her and escape had been quickly smoldered.

I walked slowly to the bathroom, thankful to be free from the chair and moving my legs which were achy from sitting so long. As I stepped inside the small guest bathroom, I went to close the door when I felt it hit something and bounce open. I looked down to see Cindy's foot blocking the door from closing, her face smug as I looked up at her, confused.

"Can I have some privacy?" I asked even though I already knew the answer.

"I don't see why you would need it. It's not like I haven't had to sit here and listen to you moan while you and Noah fuck each other. So no, you don't deserve any privacy when you openly flaunted your relationship with him to make me jealous." She pointed the gun toward the toilet and nodded for me to do my business. A blush crept up my neck as I thought about her listening to Noah and I having sex.

I took a deep breath as I struggled with what to do. I desperately needed to use the restroom, but I was beyond uncomfortable doing so in front of Cindy while she watched me. It was completely embarrassing and humiliating but as I watched her, my eyes silently pleading with hers, I knew that she wasn't going to budge. She was determined to degrade me and humiliate me any way she could.

Slowly I pulled down my pants and underwear, and squatted down onto the toilet seat, careful to keep my legs closed as I used my hand to shield myself from her view. My heart was racing as I watched her stare at me, a smirk on her face as she watched me struggle to keep what privacy I could as I used the bathroom. I finished quickly and flushed the toilet as I turned away from her and pulled my pants up in record time. I washed my hands and dried them while she watched my every move, the gun still fixated on me.

She stepped out of the way as I walked to the door, allowing me to walk in front of her as we walked down the short hallway back into the living room and kitchen area. I contemplated whether to run for it, take off and pray that I could make it to the door before she could fire off a round, but part of me didn't put it past her to have a good aim.

"I came in second in a marksmanship contest back home, so trust me when I say that I will have a bullet in the back of your head before you even reach the door," she warned as if reading my thoughts. I walked the rest of the way and turned to face her once we were in the living room. I didn't want to voluntarily go back and be tied to the chair if I didn't have to, but I also had no idea what Cindy had in store for me. It wasn't like she could just keep me here forever.

"Sit." She pointed to the chair with the gun and raised her eyebrows as she waited for me to move.

"Do you really feel it's necessary to keep me tied to the chair? You said it yourself, you can put a bullet in the back of my head before I even make it to the door." I gave her a knowing look as I challenged her to question her own ability. One thing I learned growing up in a home where nothing was ever stable was that manipulation could get you where you needed to go.

"Maybe I just like to see you suffer," she snapped at me, tapping her foot on the carpet as she waited for me to respond.

"Maybe. But I don't think that's it." I let out a dramatic sigh as if I was already bored with the conversation. I saw her expression change to curiosity and knew that I had her exactly where I wanted her.

"Oh really? And why would you think that?" She shifted her weight and tilted her head to the side. "What if I want nothing more than to watch you suffer?"

"Then you would have done something besides tie me to a chair. You've had me in your apartment almost 24 hours now. If you were going to do something, you would've done it."

"Don't act like you know what I will and won't do. You don't know me at all. You don't have any idea of what I'm capable of."

"Maybe not. But I can see that you're a good person, Cindy. You don't want to hurt me or make me suffer. You just wanted me out of the way with Noah. I get it. But you're not a mean person Cindy, you don't like to hurt people if you don't have to."

Her expression softened as I saw her shoulders drop some as if the words that I spoke somehow lifted a weight off her shoulders.

"So, do you think that we can agree that I won't try to run if you don't tie me to that chair again? You can shoot me if I try to." I forced a smile as I waited for her to give in and accept what I was offering.

"Fine. But if you get anywhere near that door or try to scream again, I'll put two bullets in your head." She walked to the counter and picked up her cell phone as she sat the gun on the counter where her phone had been.

I let out a heavy sigh as I walked over and sat on the couch, hoping that I would figure out a way to get out of this mess. The longer I was here, the harder it was getting.

Thirty One
Noah

"Do you want to talk about it?" Chase asked as he stood outside my office and leaned against the doorway. It was too early on a Monday morning to have to think about any of this, especially since I hadn't slept well last night and started having nightmares about Jade again.

"There's nothing to talk about. She said it's over, so it's over." I slammed my mouse down beside my computer and pushed my chair back as I stood up.

"So it's over? Just like that?" Chase stepped back to let me pass as I walked by without looking at him.

"Yeah, just like that," I snapped, grinding my jaw.

"What the fuck happened to you?"

I whipped around and turned to face him as anger flashed across my face, our bodies inches away from each other as I balled my fists at my sides.

"You have a lot of nerve, you know that?" I growled. "You think you get to come in here and question me about my relationship, or lack of one? She left ME, Chase. What do you expect me to do? Chase her? Force her to be with me? She doesn't want to be with me so I have no choice but to let her go."

He squared his shoulders as he took a deep breath and I waited for the first punch to be thrown. We rarely ever got in each other's faces like this but when we did, it almost always came to blows.

"Maybe if you would fight harder for her, she wouldn't have left."

"You think I didn't fight for her? You have no fucking idea how hard I've been fighting for her! She found the fucking engagement ring and she STILL left!" My voice boomed through the narrow hallway and I was thankful that no one else was around to hear it.

"She knew you were going to propose?" He took a step back and crossed his arms over his chest.

"Yeah, she had seen it Saturday morning when she came over to talk. I had cleaned everything else up before she got there but I forgot about the ring and she found it." I let out a heavy breath, feeling the anger slowly leave my body.

"What did she say?"

"She asked me what it was for. We didn't get into it, I wanted to try to keep everything a secret for Sunday. But then she didn't show up and sent me a text saying she was leaving town so we could have a clean break." I leaned back against the wall and tilted my head backward as I looked up at the ceiling.

"I'm sorry. I didn't know that she already knew about the ring. I thought maybe she just assumed that you weren't ready to settle down, that's why she didn't show up. Mia thought maybe Jade was worried that you were trying to force things to work because you were stressed about everything with Cindy."

"Has Mia talked to her?" My heartbeat started to race as I hoped that Mia might have some information as to what was going on with Jade.

"No, she hasn't heard from her. She tried calling her all day yesterday, but she hasn't answered. We just assumed that maybe she was upset about everything that was happening between you guys and that's why she hasn't been answering. We know that she probably feels out of place with everything, given that Mia and I have known you for so long. Jade has never kept it a secret that she's felt out of place with the childhood stories we share and that we've all known each other most of our lives."

"I don't know what to do." I sighed heavily and looked him in the eyes. "What do I do? How do I make her see that she's the only person that I want?"

"I don't know. But I wish I did." He smiled sympathetically at me as he leaned against the opposite wall. We both stayed silent for a few minutes, both at a loss of words.

"Maybe it's not too late," I blurted out.

"What's not?"

"Fighting for her." I pushed off from the wall and felt my face heat up as a smile stretched across my face. "I'm going to keep fighting until I can make her see how much I love her. If she still decides it's not enough after that, then I'll at least go to my grave knowing that I tried."

"I know that look on your face, what are you about to do?" he asked as he followed me to my office.

"True love has no boundaries my friend, and I'm about to show her just how true my love really is."

I chuckled as he lowered his head into his hands and groaned.

"You got things covered here today?" I asked as I grabbed my cell phone and keys off my desk.

"Do I have a choice?" He raised his eyebrows as he watched me fly past him out of the office and down the hall.

"Nope," I called over my shoulder before the door slammed behind me.

Thirty Two
Jade

It was after nine in the morning when I heard Cindy calling in to work, complaining that she was feeling under the weather and wouldn't be able to make it in. I had no idea what she had planned and figured that she would just tie me to the chair again while she went to work. The fact that she had called in instead made me worry about what she had in mind since she couldn't afford to call in every day just to stay here and make sure I didn't leave. My nerves were starting to feel fried when I thought about how much longer all of this could keep going on.

Last night had been different and thankfully she hadn't tied me up again after our quick talk about her being able to put a bullet in my head if I tried to leave. I was allowed to sit on the couch and go to the bathroom when needed, with her escorting me, of course. But aside from that, I wasn't allowed to do anything else. A single glass of water to last me the entire day and a few sandwiches to count as lunch and dinner. By the time night fell, she was tired and cranky, which meant she wasn't easy to manipulate and I had been bound to the chair again for the entire night.

My body was sore this morning, but I was relieved to not be tied up to the chair for a little bit while Cindy ate her omelet and I nibbled on the toast she gave me. I was feeling optimistic that maybe today would be the day that I could get through to her and convince her to let me go but part of me knew that wasn't going to happen. I knew that I could manipulate her based on what I had been able to do so far, but she was far from stupid, and I wasn't that skilled with manipulating others.

Shortly after she called in, I saw her grab the rope from the kitchen table and head toward me. Dread filled my stomach as I eyed it.

"Come on, let's go. To the chair." She stood next to it and held out the rope as she waited. I contemplated whether or not to push my luck. To tell her no. As if reading my mind, she reached behind her and grabbed the gun, pointing it at me until I got up and walked over to the chair. A few minutes later I was bound to the chair again, my energy feeling depleted.

"I'm going to go take a shower, and I need you to make sure you're on your very best behavior," she mocked as she wrapped the bandana around my face, forcing it into my mouth before tying it tightly behind my head. I let out a frustrated breath through my nose and glared at her as she walked around and leaned forward to look at me. "There we go, that should do." She smiled a smug smile and walked off down the hallway, the sound of the shower turning on a few seconds later.

I leaned my head back against the back of the chair and closed my eyes. This was pure hell and I needed to find a way out of it. The sound of water from the bathroom softly filled the room and I was thankful for a break from having her in the room with me. Her energy was toxic, and I felt like it clouded my brain, making it almost impossible to think of a way to outthink her and get out of this mess.

My eyes were still closed as I tried to focus on clearing my mind when I heard faint voices outside. I opened my eyes and tried to lean as far forward as I could so I could try to hear better. My heart skipped a beat when I heard Noah's voice.

"Hey, Chaz, is Jade home?"

"She hasn't been home since I got here Saturday night."

"What do you mean she hasn't been home since Saturday night?"

I could hear the anger in Noah's voice as he got louder which worked in my favor as I continued to listen.

"I mean that I haven't seen her in the apartment since Saturday night. She's not here."

"Did she leave a note or anything?"

"Nope."

I heard the door shut and disappointment flooded through me. Noah was so close yet there was nothing I could do to tell him I was in here. I pulled as hard as I could against the ropes, the thick material cutting deeper into the marks that were already on my wrists from the last time I tried this. I screamed as loud as I could under the bandana, forcing as much air out as I could but nothing actually came out. I was starting to panic as I pulled harder, almost knocking myself and the chair over. I heard heavy pounding and stilled.

"What?" Chaz's voice was filled with irritation.

"I know she's in here. I don't know why you're lying to me, but I know she's here."

I heard a loud thud as the door slammed against the wall.

"Jade! I know you're here, just come out and talk to me. Please. Jade!" I heard Noah's voice fading as he walked around inside my apartment. A few seconds later I heard banging as he knocked on my bedroom door.

"Jade, please open the door and talk to me. I know that you're upset about something and I really want to talk about it."

My heart was aching as I heard him pleading with me through the door, not knowing that I wasn't on the other side.

"I will do whatever you need me to, so you'll forgive me. Just tell me what it is, and I'll do it."

Tears ran down my face as I screamed into the bandana and tried to pull against the ropes. I was shaking so hard that I hadn't noticed Cindy come in until she was standing beside me, scowling as she watched. Her attention shifted to the wall that we shared, and she walked closer as she heard Noah's voice from the other side.

"I'm not leaving until you talk to me Jade, I know you're in there. I'm not giving up on us, not until you tell me to my face that I'm no longer the man you love."

I closed my eyes and lowered my head as the tears continued to run down my face.

"Looks like we need to fix this little problem, don't we?" Cindy walked back over to me and forced my head up by yanking my hair down and holding it tight so I couldn't move my head.

I tried to keep listening to what was happening on the other side of the wall, but I couldn't hear Noah's voice anymore. A few minutes later I heard a door slam closed and knew that he had left. Cindy's lips turned upward into a devious smile as she heard the sound and turned to glare at me before letting go of my hair. I took a deep breath and tried to force myself to relax but was caught off guard when Cindy was behind me again, pulling my hair down and forcing my head back into the same position.

I watched as I caught a glimpse of something silver out of the corner of my eye. Within seconds I felt something cold skim the back of my neck and heard the scissors as they cut through my hair. She turned to look at me, holding a massive amount of blonde hair in her hands before dropping it to the floor beside me.

Thirty Three
Noah

Irritation continued to course through my veins as I left Jade's apartment, the image of Chaz's smug smile still fresh in my mind. I pulled into the parking lot of The Vine and put the truck in park as I contemplated what I wanted to do. I had never been in this kind of situation before and it was driving me crazy that I couldn't figure out what to do. Everything I did seemed to be the wrong thing. If this was what love was actually supposed to be like, I now understood why most people complained about how hard it actually was.

I leaned forward and rested my arm on the steering wheel as I thought through the options I had. I could go inside and try to work, pretending nothing had happened while I obsessed over Jade all day. Or I could go see the one person who knew the most about love and even more about heartache.

Fifteen minutes later I pulled up in front of Grant's house, knowing he would be home since the school he worked at was closed because of the weather. I knocked on the door as I pulled my beanie down lower on my head as the cold wind blew past me sending a chill through me.

"Hey, what's up?" Grant stepped back as he opened the door for me to come inside.

"Sorry to just drop in." I wiped my feet several times on the doormat before going in to make sure my boots didn't track in snow. "I was hoping we could talk?"

"Is this a beer at ten o'clock in the morning talk or will coffee do?" he called from the kitchen as I closed the door behind me and followed him inside.

"Coffee would be great, thanks."

I heard footsteps running down the stairs and looked over to see Liam fly around the corner in the flannel pajamas that Jade had bought him for Christmas.

"Good morning, Liam," I said as he came in and hopped up onto the barstool at the island, pouring himself a glass of orange juice before turning and waving at me as he drank it.

I took a seat at the kitchen table and watched as Grant and Liam moved around each other as Grant made coffee and Liam slipped around him to sneak a donut out of the box on the counter before running off to the living room. I chuckled and shook my head, knowing that Liam was exactly the same as how his dad was at his age.

A few minutes later the coffee finished brewing and Grant brought two cups over to the table and sat across from me as he handed me my cup. He slowly sipped his while eyeing me over the rim, waiting for me to spill it on why I was at his house on a Monday morning when I should be at work.

I wanted to dive right in and tell him everything, brainstorm ideas with him on how to fix everything, but the problem was that I didn't even know what I was trying to fix. Jade left me and I honestly didn't know why. He let out a heavy sigh as he took another sip before setting his cup down in front of him and leaned back against the padded chair and watched me.

"I don't know where to start," I muttered as I kept my eyes fixated on the coffee mug in front of me on the table.

"Well then I'm not sure how much help I can be." He licked his lips as a smile crept its way onto his face. "We could always start from the beginning."

I looked up at him and found a playful smile on his face as his hand stretched out across the table, fingers tapping along the worn-out wooden top.

"You know the beginning. Things between Jade and I were fucking awesome at the beginning."

"I meant from the beginning, like when you were ten and you kissed Linda Thompson when you knew that I liked her. I think that's where everything started to go downhill for you."

I let out a laugh as I leaned back in my chair and shook my head.

"You're never going to let that go, are you? She was too young for you, and honestly, you didn't have my skills." I winked as I pretended to pop my collar, something we had done from the moment someone had said it was cool.

"Hey, I could have had her if I really wanted her. But no, you had to go and kiss her. Turn her into a lesbian." His smile was contagious, and I was thankful for the lighthearted banter.

"Don't blame that one on me!" I put my hands up in surrender. "It was one kiss, that was it! But you know, I heard that Maggie ended up kissing her after I did, and honestly, I think that was her turning point." I smiled as I remembered such distant memories.

"Maggie could have turned anyone, she was drop-dead gorgeous."

"They both were."

We sighed at the same time and when I looked back up at him I found comfort in his eyes as he waited for me to talk about the real issue.

"Jade left me," I blurted out as I looked down and spun my spoon in a circle on the table.

"I'm sorry, man. Chase told me that she never showed up yesterday for brunch and that she sent a text instead. What happened?" He picked up his cup and took a drink, his eyes never leaving my face.

"Honestly? I have no fucking idea." I exhaled loudly and pushed the spoon to the side as I turned to face him directly.

"What did the message say?"

"Not much other than she didn't want to lead me on so she was going to leave town so we'd have a clean break."

"Ouch." He flinched subtly.

"Yeah."

"All of this just happened out of the blue after she came over to talk to you the day before?"

"She literally left my house smiling and held onto my hand for a minute as she walked out the door. We had talked about Cindy and the ultrasound, we even talked about her living with Chaz. None of that changed how we were while she was there. I don't see what could have changed after she left when we literally sat down and had a handful of tough conversations before she agreed to come over yesterday. I can't imagine her saying yes to brunch if she was upset with me."

Grant nodded his head as he followed along and sipped his coffee.

"Have you tried to talk to her since?"

"Yeah, I tried calling and texting her Saturday night to see if we were still on for Sunday but she didn't respond. So I thought maybe she was at Mia's, having dinner like they had originally planned before that storm hit. I asked Mia and she said Jade wasn't there and offered to go check on her."

"So why not ask Mia for an update?"

"That's the thing, Mia said that Jade wasn't home." I swallowed past the lump that was starting to form in my throat. "So I decided to go by Jade's apartment this morning to talk to her, and according to Chaz, he hasn't seen her since he got home Saturday night."

Grant's brow pulled together as he took the information in and I was relieved that he felt the same way I did about it.

"That's weird. Has she been at work?"

"Nope. I went by SlowMo's and Arlene said that Jade had the weekend off. She's supposed to go in at four tonight for the dinner shift."

"So are you here to officially ask me out to dinner?" A smile tugged at the corner of his lips and I felt mine follow.

"Well, it has been a while since I've been on an actual date. I guess I could lower my standards some," I joked.

"Maybe she just needs some time? It's only been a few days since you talked to her on Saturday, maybe something else came up."

"Maybe, but it just doesn't feel right. This isn't like Jade and it's driving me crazy that it's so out of the blue. She was fine on Saturday. She would have shown up on Sunday but something got in her way and I can't figure out what."

"Well, I wish I could offer you some advice on that but I feel just as clueless as you. I would love to be able to tell you how to fix it but the only thing I've got is to give her time and space. If that's what this is then it will sort itself out."

I blew out a breath as I tapped my foot on the tiled floor, shaking my head before I turned to look at him again.

"You know I can't do that, right?"

"Yeah."

"So I'll meet you at SlowMo's at six?"

"We'll be there."

He let out a laugh as I finished my cup of coffee and headed off to work.

The day went by at an incredibly slow pace given that we were dead with everyone staying home due to the weather. I was sitting at one of the tables in the back working on some paperwork when I heard the bell chime on the front door. I looked over to see blonde hair walking up toward the bar area and got excited that Jade had given in and come by to talk to me.

Julia pointed in my direction from behind the bar and I smiled as I waited for her to turn around, completely disappointed when I saw Cindy making her way toward me. She was grinning from ear to ear as she waddled toward me and I made a mental note to ask Jade to change her hair color the next time I saw her.

"Hey Noah, how's it going?" she asked as she leaned in and tried to hug me. I watched her with a blank look on my face as my body refused to touch her. Her face fell and her smile was replaced with a frown before she pulled out the stool next to me and sat down.

I raised an eyebrow as I watched her, moving the papers that were scattered across the table out of the way.

"What do you want, Cindy?" Annoyance heavy in my tone.

"I wanted to let you know that I got in touch with the clinic back home, and they were able to send over the original ultrasounds to the doctor's office. I have another appointment on Friday. Maybe you can come with me again?" Her voice got higher as she practically squealed.

"I don't think so, sorry." I lowered my head to focus on the report I was working on before she interrupted me. Sometimes I liked to get out of my office to work on things but today it seemed like it would have been better to be cooped up inside the four walls that felt like they were closing in than to sit with Cindy.

"I can reschedule it if another day works better for you?" She reached over and gently squeezed my arm, bringing my attention back to her. I pulled my arm away from her, letting her hand fall on the table in its absence.

"Don't worry about it, just keep your appointment."

"But it's important to me that you be there, Noah."

"Look, Cindy, I have a lot of work to do and I'm not interested in going to the appointments with you anymore. We have nothing left to say, so if you don't mind, I have work to do." I gave her a pointed look before turning my attention back to the papers in front of me.

I watched as she stood up and pushed her stool in before walking behind me. I let out a loud sigh as I waited for her to leave, startled when I felt her behind me. Her hands ran down my chest and over my stomach as she leaned down behind me. I could feel the warmth from her body as her stomach pushed into me, her breasts pressed into my back.

"What do you think you're doing?" I demanded as my hands reached up and grabbed hers, holding them in place so they'd stop wondering down my body. There was no one else around but it still felt beyond inappropriate, even for me.

"You seem really stressed, I could help you with that," she whispered as her lips hovered by my ear. Her tongue ran down the side of my neck as she shifted and forced her breasts to rub along my back. I could feel her hands trying to get out from under mine as I quickly flung them around and spun myself out of her reach.

"I don't need your help with anything, I need you to stop."

"No one has to know, we can do it right here. It could be our little secret." She licked her lips as she started to bend down to climb under the table.

"Cindy, no."

"You can't tell me that you wouldn't enjoy my lips around your thick cock again. I still remember the way it stretched my mouth as I sucked it, pulling you all the way to my throat." She stepped closer as I kept my grip on her hands. "You don't have to do anything, just use my body however you want it. If you don't want to come in my mouth, you could always come on my tits. They're nice and big right now." She looked down and pulled her hand free as she ran a finger along the top of the low cut shirt that was barely containing her breasts.

I shook my head as I tried to turn away but as her fingers dipped lower into her shirt, a glimpse of her bra showed. It was a black lace bra with tiny red flowers, just like the one Jade had. I looked closer at the shirt she was wearing and noticed that it was super tight and didn't seem to fit, just like the bra that was barely containing her. The shirt was a black workout tank top that I had seen Jade wear plenty of times, including when I saw her on Saturday.

"Is that Jade's shirt and bra?" I asked as I stared dumbly at her, praying that she hadn't gone that crazy to go out and buy the same clothes as Jade.

"Of course not!" she exclaimed with a tone that sounded forced. "Why on earth would you even ask that?"

"Jade has a bra just like that. And she wears shirts like that all the time."

"Well then maybe she's been copying me?" A smug look landed on her face as she watched for my reaction.

"Yeah, maybe." I turned my attention back to the pile of stuff on the table in front of me and quickly worked to pile it up before turning and walking away from Cindy.

Thirty Four
Jade

I was sitting in the chair, bound to it once again, but this time I had the added humiliation of being topless. I had no idea what to expect next from Cindy after she lost her mind hearing Noah in my apartment this morning. There was a cold chill in the apartment and I didn't know if it was because I was completely exposed from the waist up, or if it was from being in shock still.

After Cindy cut my hair, I was in total disbelief that she would do something like that. But then I saw her wave my hair around like some sort of prize and I knew that she was completely crazy. She muttered to herself about needing to take it one step further, that's all she needed and Noah would finally start looking at her the way he looked at me.

She went to the bedroom and got ready but as she was about to walk out the door, she changed her mind and closed it softly before walking over and picking up the gun. While keeping it aimed at my head, she forced me to give her my shirt and bra, then insisted that I didn't deserve to have anything else to wear. I was mortified when I saw her change into it, wearing the clothes that I had been wearing as she struggled to fit them over her pregnant body. The workout top was stretchy but only to a point. When added with a bra that was too small for her, her cleavage was pushed up and over the top, making her look like a very pregnant, cheap prostitute.

It had been about an hour since she left according to the time on the microwave. I eyed the gun still sitting on the counter where she left it and contemplated whether I could get to it before she got back. If I could somehow find a way to hide it from her, then I could try to overpower her the next time she untied me without having to worry about her shooting me. Even though I knew it was damn near impossible to do anything while I was bound to a chair, it was the only hope that I had left.

A few minutes later I heard a key in the door and grunted in disappointment that she was back. I waited for the door to open but it didn't. Outside I could hear faint voices and tilted my head to try to hear. I could easily make out Cindy's annoying voice, but the other voice, the one she was talking to, was soft and feminine. Mia.

My heart started racing as I imagined Cindy doing something to Mia and prayed that she would just let her be. I held my breath and tried to calm myself so the pounding in my ears from my racing pulse would stop and allow me to hear what was happening.

"Hey, Mia. How's it going?"

"I'm fine, thank you." Mia's voice was further away so I had to strain to hear it.

"Are you looking for Jade?"

"Yeah, I was hoping to talk to her before she goes to work."

I waited to see what Cindy would say, knowing that Mia would know no one was home when I didn't answer the door. I had heard Chaz leave shortly after Cindy left earlier and knew he wouldn't be back until after he got off of work.

"Jade's not home, I saw her leave this morning."

"You did? Do you know where she was going?"

"She didn't say. But she looked like she had been crying and she had her suitcase. It looked pretty full."

My heart sank.

"Oh, that's right, I remember now. She did say she was going out of town for a few days to see her mother. I completely forgot. Thanks for letting me know, I'll touch base with her when she gets back."

I was thankful for Mia's quick thinking even though I knew she had no idea what was really going on. She trusted her instincts and that meant she would be safe from Cindy.

"No problem." Cindy's voice was overly cheerful and I let out a heavy sigh knowing Mia should be walking away and going home.

"Hey Mia," Cindy called out. "I would love to get together sometime, maybe have some girl time, if you're free?"

"Yeah, I'll have to check my calendar. Things have been busy with the baby and my maternity leave is almost over."

"Okay. I just wanted to see if we could sit down and talk about things with Noah and me. I feel bad about everything that's happened and he won't listen to me anymore. Even after I told him that the doctor from the other clinic sent over the original ultrasounds and lab results."

"I don't think I should be getting involved Cindy, I'm sorry. I'm sure you guys will figure it out."

"I hope so, I would hate to lose him in his baby's life over something so silly."

I cringed as I listened to their conversation and silently pleaded with Mia to just walk and leave before it was too late.

"Well, I better get going. Rylee is going to need a nap soon."

Thank the lord. Go, Mia, walk away.

I heard the key in the door once more and waited for her to unlock the door.

"Oh hey, Cindy, do you think I can get those pictures back that you borrowed since I'm here?"

I closed my eyes and shook my head.

"I haven't made copies of them yet, can I bring them by in a few days?"

"If you show me which ones they are, I don't mind printing copies and bringing them back to you," Mia pushed as her voice got louder and I knew she was walking closer to the apartment.

"I couldn't put that extra work on you. I'll go out and get the copies made today and I'll drop them off tonight. I'm feeling a little tired so I need to get inside and rest."

I could hear the aggressive tone in Cindy's voice and prayed that Mia heard it as well and backed off.

"Okay, that's fine. I'll see you tonight."

I heard footsteps as Mia walked away and a few seconds later Cindy walked in, looking furious. She had a plastic bag on her arm as she slammed the door shut and glared at me.

"Looks like we're going to have to deal with you sooner than I thought."

She stalked over to me and my eyes went wide as I watched her lift the skillet from the stove and swing it at my head. The pain was radiating as my head whipped back and everything went quiet.

Thirty Five
Noah

I waited in my truck at SlowMo's for Grant and Liam to show up, feeling uneasy that Jade's car wasn't in the parking lot. A few minutes later I saw his truck pull up beside me and we all got out and went inside. It was busier than I had expected for a Monday night but we were seated right away and taken to a table in the back. As we were walking back, I let out a chuckle when I saw that Chase and Mia were sitting at the table next to where they were seating us.

"Apparently this is the place to be tonight," I joked as I bent down to hug Mia before patting Chase's shoulder.

"We decided it would be nice to get out for a bite to eat tonight," Chase said as he eyed Mia.

Grant and Liam sat down at the table as I pulled off my jacket and hung it on the back of my chair. I bent down to kiss Rylee on her head while she slept in her car seat before sitting down to join everyone.

"No, we came to check on Jade." Mia's voice was filled with tension as she leaned forward and rested her arms on the table in front of her. Chase pulled his mouth into a thin line and turned to look at his wife.

"I thought we weren't going to say anything?" he asked her quietly even though we could all hear.

"It's fine, it's the same reason that we're here." I pointed to Grant and Liam and looked directly at Mia. Something had happened that made her concerned and I was going to find out what it was.

"Have you seen her?" I asked her directly before my eyes shifted to scan the room.

"No, and Arlene said that she hasn't shown up for her shift. She was supposed to be here at four." Mia sighed heavily and leaned back as a waitress reached across her to set the glasses of water on the table for her and Chase.

"Something's not right," I said to no one in particular.

"Maybe she's sick, there's no reason to freak out right away," Grant spoke softly as he sat a menu in front of Liam to look at.

"I doubt she's sick." I tapped my foot anxiously and looked around once again, hoping she would somehow just appear.

"I agree, she's not sick." Mia leaned back against the chair and studied me.

"How do you know?" Chase asked as he rocked the car seat to keep Rylee asleep.

"Because I went to go see her today."

"You went to see her?" Chase's eyebrows shot up as he turned in his seat to look at her.

"Yes. I was worried."

"And you didn't bother to tell me until now?"

"You would have told me not to go."

"You're damn right I would have."

I watched as they stared at each other, neither of them giving.

"So what happened when you went to see her?" I asked, needing to know everything I could.

"She wasn't home." Mia folded her hands on top of each other as she sat them on the table in front of her.

"How do you know?" My eyes searched hers as I waited.

"No one answered the door. But her car was there."

"Maybe we need to ask her landlord to let us in? Demand a welfare check? What if she's really sick?" My voice was getting higher as panic started to rush through me.

"Don't you think Chaz would know if something was wrong with her? After all, she's not living there by herself anymore." Chase spoke calmly as he looked at me.

"Chaz told me he hasn't seen her since he's been home Saturday night." I shifted in my chair and nodded no to the waitress as she approached. I didn't care how hungry anyone was, I needed to know what was going on.

"Okay, so who was the last person to see her?" Grant asked as he passed his phone to Liam to let him play a game while we talked. There were packets of crackers on the table that he slid over to him as well.

"I saw her Saturday afternoon when she came over and I haven't heard from her since." I chewed my lower lip as my feet felt like they were going to take off from tapping so quickly.

"According to Cindy, she saw her today."

"What?" I narrowed my eyes at her as she said Cindy's name. Everyone's eyes were now on Mia, waiting for an explanation.

"She told me that Jade wasn't there. That she had left earlier with a suitcase and looked like she had been crying."

I felt like my world was collapsing around me, the words trapped in my throat.

"What else did Cindy say?" Chase asked with a stern tone in his voice.

"Nothing about Jade. I pretended that Jade had told me she was leaving for a few days, that she was going to go see her mom. Then Cindy asked about hanging out and wanting to talk about things with Noah. I told her that I didn't think it was a good idea for me to get involved. She was acting weird and I couldn't put my finger on it, so I asked if I could get the pictures back that she borrowed. She didn't want to let me in the apartment, so I kept trying." Mia shrugged her shoulders and looked away from the table, avoiding the pissed off look she was getting from Chase.

"You did that when you had Rylee with you?" Chase asked, his finger reaching across and pulling Mia's face back toward his.

"She was safe, I had her wrapped around me in her sling."

"Mia! Do you have any fucking idea how much danger you put her in today? How much danger you put yourself in?!" Chase's voice boomed around us, causing the others sitting near us to turn around and look.

"We were fine, Chase, I knew what I was doing," she snapped.

"No, Mia, obviously you didn't. If you thought Jade was in trouble, you should have come to me. I would have gone to check on her. You don't go putting yourself, or our daughter, in harm's way."

"I was fine! She's my best friend, Chase, and she risked her life to save me from Damian. I owe it to her to save her from whatever the hell is happening!" Her voice broke at the end and we watched as the tears ran down her face as she pulled away when Chase tried to hold her.

"I know Mia, I'm sorry. I just, I can't stand the thought of anything happening to you or the baby." Chase reached over and pulled her into him, holding her as she wiped her eyes.

"So what do we do now?" Grant asked.

"I have no idea." I ran a hand through my hair and prayed for a sign that would tell me where she was.

"Did Jade really talk to you about leaving town for a few days?" Grant asked Mia.

"No, we hadn't talked about her leaving, and as far as I know she never had any plans to leave. She was happy to be here and finally putting some roots down. I just made that up to see how Cindy would react since she told me Jade left."

"In the message that I got from Jade on Sunday, after she stood me up, it mentioned that she was leaving town so we could have a clean break."

"Do you really think she would just up and leave?" Chase asked as he kept an arm wrapped around Mia's shoulders.

"I don't know. Maybe? She's talked about her childhood and how every time her mom ended a relationship, they would leave town. Maybe she's just doing the only thing she knows how to do."

I looked across the table at Mia and saw the sadness on her face. As much as I didn't want to believe it, I knew that I was right.

Thirty Six
Jade

I woke up to a throbbing headache and was surprised that I wasn't bound to the chair. I looked around and saw an empty room, knowing it was the guest bedroom in Cindy's apartment. The layout of her apartment was opposite of mine which meant that our master bedrooms shared a wall, and her guest bedroom was at the other end. Given that her apartment was the last one on this floor, there were no neighbors to share a wall with. I could scream as loud as I wanted to in this room and no one would hear me.

I sat up and looked down, thankful that I now had a T-shirt on and was no longer naked from the top up. It was a ratty worn-out T-shirt and part of me prayed that it wasn't something Cindy had recently worn. I would almost rather that she pulled it out of a dumpster than to wear something she had worn. She was pure evil, and I didn't want anything from her on me.

I ran a hand through my hair out of habit and felt my stomach drop when I felt how short my hair was. When I first moved here my hair was rather short, but this was even shorter and not by any means straight. I cringed at the thought of how horrible my hair looked and wondered just how uneven it was. There was a strong chemical smell that lingered on my fingers from touching my hair and I tried to figure out what it was. Then it clicked from the numerous times I had colored my hair on my own. Store-bought hair dye. I groaned as I thought about how I had no idea what she had done while I was passed out.

I heard footsteps approaching and watched as the door handle turned before the door opened and Cindy walked in.

"You're finally awake I see," she said as she walked over and brought the chair and rope in with her. I stayed quiet, not having the energy to try to figure out what to say to her. My body felt like it had been run over by a truck and I feared that I had been hit with more than just the skillet that knocked me out. She smiled as if reading my thoughts.

"I got you a few things that you'll need when you leave, but I'm still waiting for your ride to come pick you up."

"What are you talking about?" I asked, my voice barely above a whisper.

"You're leaving town, just like you've told everyone you were. And now, thanks to me, no one will recognize you as you go."

I watched as she stood there, looking me over.

"I'm not going anywhere." Why was my body so weak? I felt like every tiny bit of strength I had had been pulled out of me and stripped away.

"Of course you are. And I have a friend from back home who will be escorting you just to make sure you don't get any ideas about trying to come back."

I rolled my eyes as I looked up at her, the look on her face changing as she glared at me. A second later her fist landed on my cheek, knocking me back down to the floor. I struggled to get up, but it was impossible as her foot kicked me over and over. I laid where I was, curled up in a fetal position as I prayed it would stop.

Thirty Seven
Noah

The room was dark as I crept along the wall, staying hidden in the shadows as I tried to get to Jade. I could hear her whimpering, knowing she was in pain. Each step I took forward felt like I was further away, the sound of her cries fading in the distance. I tried to walk faster, desperate to get to her. Soon I was running, faster, until I was out of breath. I got close enough to see her, her face covered in blood. My hand reached out to grab hers, to pull her up off the floor, but when I touched her it was no longer Jade. Staring back at me was Cindy.

My eyes flew open, my breathing rapid as my heart raced out of control. I sat up in bed and pulled the covers off of me as I got up and went to the kitchen for a glass of water. The nightmares about Jade weren't unusual, but tonight's really got to me. There was something about it that felt like more than just a bad dream. It felt like it was real.

I glanced at the clock on the stove, confirming that I was up for the day. It was already five in the morning and I didn't feel like going back to sleep for another hour and having more nightmares. I started a pot of coffee before making my way to the guest room to work out before heading in to work. At this rate, I would soon be in the physical shape I had been wanting to be in for a few months now with all of the extra lifting sessions I was adding in as a stress reliever for everything going on with Jade and Cindy.

A few hours later I was in my office working on a report when I heard voices from Chase's office. I kept my head down and tried to focus on the information in front of me but as the voices grew louder, my focus became nonexistent. I shoved the paper away as I stood up and walked out of my office to see what all of the fuss was about in his.

"I don't care what everyone says, I know better. Something is wrong, I can feel it," Mia whispered loudly as she sat on the edge of Chase's desk and faced him. I cleared my throat as I leaned against the doorway and crossed my arms across my chest. They both looked at me at the same time, a faint blush creeping up Mia's neck as she turned to look at me.

"Everything alright in here?" I asked as I looked between them.

"Yeah, everything is fine." Chase sighed heavily.

Mia's eyes locked onto mine and I could tell something was wrong. I'd known her long enough to know that look.

"What's up, Mia?"

She went to say something when I saw Chase's hand gently squeeze her knee, forcing her to turn her head back to him. I raised an eyebrow at him in response.

"Fine." He leaned back in his high back leather chair and laced his fingers behind his head. "Mia is convinced that something is wrong with Jade."

My eyes shifted to Mia as she turned back around and watched me. I gave her a quick nod for her to tell me why she thought something was wrong. I had been feeling like something was wrong myself but had been attributing it to the nightmares and stress with how everything ended.

"It's not like her to just leave, Noah. You know that. I know that." Her voice was quiet as she talked.

"I don't know what I know anymore." I ran a hand down the scruff on my face and let out a deep breath.

"She wouldn't just leave you, I know her better than that. If she was going to leave, she would have done it a long time ago. When you guys first broke up. But she didn't, Noah, she stayed. And since then, she's been there for you every step of the way. I was wrong last night when I thought that she would just up and leave because that's what she's been used to, I didn't give her credit for how far she's come in her relationship with you."

I watched as Mia turned around further, giving me her full attention as she spoke.

"She acknowledged that she was used to running from relationships the night you guys came for dinner and she broke it off again, but Noah, she wasn't ending it because she wanted to leave. She ended it so you didn't have to choose between her and the baby. She loved you enough to spare you that decision because she didn't want you to regret your decision if you chose her."

"How am I supposed to trust that she didn't just up and leave?"

"Because I went by her apartment this morning and her car is still there. How would she leave without her car? She loves that car, she wouldn't just abandon it."

"You went by her apartment again this morning?" I asked as I looked past her to see Chase's jaw clenched as he listened.

"Yes, I went by again. I talked to Chaz and he still hadn't seen her. He mentioned that Cindy went by on Sunday to get Jade's phone, she told him that Jade was with her building baby furniture for the nursery."

Her eyes locked onto mine as I felt a shiver run through my body. There was no way in hell that Jade would have gone over to help Cindy then send her to get her phone.

"Did he say what time on Sunday?" I asked as I swallowed down the bile that was threatening to make its way up.

"It was after noon."

I closed my eyes as I pinched the bridge of my nose and shook my head. How had I been so stupid?

"So what's your plan?"

"I want to go check out Cindy's apartment, see if anything looks odd. It took everything I had in me not to barge into her apartment this morning while I was there, but I didn't since I had the baby with me. I do think we need to seriously look into this though." Mia stood up and turned to face me.

"You can't just show up at her apartment, she'll know that something is up."

"No, she won't. When I talked to her yesterday, I asked her about getting the photos back that she borrowed. She was so desperate to get me away from her apartment that she promised she would go make copies and drop them off at my house last night, but she never showed up. So I can go over with the excuse of getting the photos from her." Mia rolled her eyes as she exhaled heavily. "I was so stupid not to question why she didn't want me in her apartment yesterday. I should have been thinking clearer."

"You also had our daughter with you," Chase reminded her as she shot him a look.

I let the thought roll around in my head and tried to find a flaw in it but couldn't. Mia was actually on the right path and I couldn't imagine that Cindy would be on to her.

"What about Chase? How are you going to explain why he's there? She'll think you're ganging up on her if he shows up and she'll shut you out immediately." My mouth was working faster than my mind but I hated that there was already a problem with the plan.

"Chase isn't going with me. No one is." She pulled her shoulders back as she stood taller and looked at Chase out of the corner of her eye.

My eyebrows shot up and I looked at Chase sitting there, fists clenched. There was no way in hell that he was okay with this.

"Mia, I don't think it's the best idea for you to go there by yourself. You don't know Cindy, and if we really think that she knows what happened to Jade, there's no telling what she might do."

"I appreciate the concern, I really do. But I'm not only the best option we have right now, I'm the only option. Unless you want to go in there with guns blazing, be my guest." She folded her arms over her chest and shifted her weight on her hip as she waited for me to respond. I looked at Chase, catching his attention before he could look away.

"What do you think?" I asked, already knowing what he thought.

"I hate the idea of it but I hate even more that she's right."

"Well, let's at least come up with a plan before you go running over there. I want to make sure we think through everything before we just send you into the fire."

"It's not that complicated. I'm just going to go to her apartment and ask for the photos. I'll try to get her to let me in so I don't have to stand outside in the cold. While I'm in there, I'll look for any sign of Jade and see how Cindy is acting. If I'm wrong and Jade isn't there then no harm, no foul. At least I got the photos back and I didn't make Cindy feel like we were accusing her of anything."

"And what if Jade is there? Then what do you do?" Chase asked sternly, drawing her attention back to him.

"I don't know," she whispered. "I fight until I get her out of there. I protect her the way she tried to protect me from Damian."

"So I'm supposed to tell Rylee that her mom got hurt, or worse, killed because she needed to run off on her own to go fight some crazy pregnant lunatic?"

I saw the hurt flash across her face at his words. But he was right. If Jade was there then it would be incredibly dangerous for Mia to go in by herself.

"Um, speaking of Rylee, where is she?" I asked as I looked down and noticed the car seat wasn't on the floor by Chase's desk where it usually was when she was sleeping.

"I dropped her off with my dad and Arlene after I left Jade's apartment. They've been wanting some time with her and I needed to take care of this, so it was a win-win."

"Obviously Chase and I can't both leave since we have no one to be here when we open. So, I'll go with you to Cindy's apartment, but I'll wait downstairs in my truck until I get a signal from you. That's my compromise, you don't go by yourself but you can go up to her apartment by yourself."

"Deal."

Mia leaned down and kissed Chase before grabbing her phone and jacket from his desk and following me out to my truck. I had a terrible, terrible feeling about all of this.

Thirty Eight
Jade

I came to and was still in the same room I was in when Cindy had beat me unconscious again earlier. I struggled to try to sit up but my body wouldn't allow it so I stopped trying and let myself lay where I was on the floor. I had no idea what time it was or how much time had passed since Cindy had been in here last.

The doorbell rang and I felt panic rush through me as I remembered her saying that she had a friend who was coming to take me out of town. There was a devious smile on her face when she said it and part of me wondered if I would make it to another town with this so-called friend of hers. I listened as her footsteps padded along the floor to answer the door and waited to hear a man's voice as I expected that was who would be coming.

My stomach sank when I heard Mia's voice instead. I silently pleaded with her to leave. Turn around, walk out the door, and leave. Nothing good could come about from her being here. My body laid still on the floor as I tried to lift my head enough to hear them talk.

"Hey, Mia, what are you doing here?" There was an edge to Cindy's tone and I prayed that Mia would pick up on it and just leave.

"Sorry for just stopping by, I was out running errands and thought I would swing by and grab those photos we talked about yesterday since you didn't make it by last night to drop them off."

"Oh, right. Sorry about that, I got busy and totally spaced it. Can I bring them to you later?"

"I was hoping I could just get them now since I'm already here. That way neither of us has to be out in this cold longer than necessary."

"Okay, I guess I'll get them real quick."

I could hear the sound of the door as she started to close it, followed by a loud thud.

"You don't mind if I come in while you get them, do you? It's awfully cold outside and I wouldn't want to be stuck out in this weather for too long."

"Of course not."

Cindy's tone was getting increasingly hard and I could picture her gritting her teeth as she talked. I tried to force myself up, to try to warn Mia to run and get out of there, but my body was too weak from the recent attacks.

"Thanks, you're the best," Mia said in a cheerful tone as I heard the door close.

"You can have a seat on the couch while I go look for them," Cindy offered as I heard her walk by my door on her way to the master bedroom.

"Thanks. Actually, do you mind if I use your restroom?" Mia called to her as I heard her walk away.

I didn't hear Cindy answer as I heard Mia quickly open and close the closet door before opening and closing the bathroom door. A few minutes later I heard Cindy's footsteps approaching as I watched in horror as the doorknob turned to open the door to the guest bedroom. Mia's eyes went wide in horror when she looked down and saw me on the floor, her hand flying to her mouth as she took a step closer.

"I thought you needed the bathroom?" Cindy asked as she stood behind Mia, the skillet flying up behind Mia's head and knocking her down to the floor next to me.

"Great, looks like I have two problems to deal with," Cindy said as she bent down and rolled Mia into the room next to me. I felt tears run down my face as I looked at my best friend lying unconscious on the floor next to me.

Thirty Nine
Noah

I checked my phone for the tenth time in the five minutes since I had seen Mia walk into Cindy's apartment. My body was humming with anxiety as my foot tapped against the rubber floor mat underneath me while I waited. Part of me wanted to rush up there and burst into the apartment, make sure everything was okay, but I knew that I needed to give Mia the benefit of the doubt that everything was okay and that her plan was working.

My eyes shifted over to movement across the parking lot as I saw Chaz get out of his car and take the stairs two at a time up to the apartment. I wanted to go confront him and ask him where the fuck she was but his story had been the same with everyone else as it was with me which made me believe that he really didn't know where she was.

Ten minutes turned into twenty minutes since Mia had gone inside and I had practically chewed a hole through my cheek with each second that had passed. I got a text message from Chase asking for an update and sent him one back confirming that I hadn't seen Mia but I was on my way up to check it out.

I hopped out of the truck and jogged across the parking lot, taking the stairs just as fast as Chaz had, feeling the adrenaline pump through me as I practically sprinted to the apartment. I knocked softly, waiting to see if I could hear anything inside. I didn't want to mess something up if Mia was actually okay and getting information, but it was eerily quiet inside which had me worried. I knocked harder and waited a few seconds when I heard footsteps and saw the door swing open as Cindy answered it.

"Hey, Noah. Now's not a good time," she said breathlessly as she wiped a bead of sweat from her forehead with her arm.

"I didn't ask if it was." I pushed past her and stormed into the apartment, searching for Mia.

"Where is she?" I demanded, watching her flinch at my tone.

"Where is who?" She pulled her brows in as she stepped around me and stood by the hallway that led to the bedrooms.

"Mia. Jade. I know they're here, tell me where they're at."

She continued to look at me like I was crazy, which sent my blood pressure even further through the roof.

"WHERE. THE. FUCK. ARE. THEY?!" I shouted as I took two steps toward her and got in her face.

"I wouldn't do that if I were you," she warned as she stood in front of the door to the guest bedroom. My eyes zeroed in on it and I knew they were inside it.

"Move out of the way, Cindy. Now!" My voice echoed through the apartment as the picture frames rattled on the wall behind me.

She narrowed her eyes at me as she stepped to the side and let me pass. I heard her walk past me into the kitchen as I opened the door and found Jade and Mia on the floor. My eyes shifted quickly back and forth between them, trying to figure out the extent of their injuries. I was furious with myself for ever letting Mia come here by herself, and even more so for not getting my ass up here quicker.

Mia groaned as she sat upright and looked at me. She nodded toward Jade as I made my way to her. I bent down and checked for a pulse. It was faint but it was there. Her body was covered in dried blood and bruises, cut marks on her wrists and arms. I leaned her head back and looked at her face. Her hair had been cut short and died brown, with spots of color missing. I cradled her head in my hand as I used the other to pull my cell phone out to call for help.

"I wouldn't do that," Cindy warned as she came in and stood behind me, a gun pointed at my head. "Step away from her now or I'll put a bullet in your friend's head." She quickly pointed the gun at Mia before turning back to point it at my head. As she moved, I noticed a necklace hanging on top of the sweater she was wearing. I looked closer and my stomach sank when I saw the locket Jade's sister had given her, hanging from Cindy's neck. I slowly sat my phone down on the carpet next to Jade and raised my hands in front of me as I watched her.

"What are you doing, Cindy?" I asked calmly as I studied her while keeping an eye on both girls without her noticing.

"I'm fixing what you screwed up. I'm making things right."

"Okay, and what's that?"

"We're supposed to be together, Noah. We're having a baby. Starting our family. But how can we do that if you're just going to keep chasing after her?" She pointed the gun at Jade and instinctively I stepped to the side to shield her. She stared at me as her jaw clenched.

"See what I mean?"

"Cindy, we can be together and be a family without you having to hurt anyone. Just let me get them help then it'll be just you and me. No one else, just us and our family."

"I don't believe you. If you call for help, they won't understand what's going on. They're going to blame me. And then we won't get to be together." Her hand shook nervously forcing me to keep my focus on the gun as I didn't trust her not to accidentally shoot it.

"We can leave, we'll get in the car and leave. Once we're gone, I'll call for an ambulance to come help them. Then no one will know anything, and we'll be gone."

"That's the most ridiculous, stupidest thing I've ever heard. You're just lying to me, telling me what you think I want to hear."

"Cindy, just give me the gun. You don't want to do this," I begged.

Her mouth turned up into a devious smile as she looked directly at me.

"Actually, I do." She turned quickly and pulled the trigger, my heart stopping as I watched the bullet fly through Mia's body. She clenched her stomach as she fell to the floor, blood pooling underneath her.

I lunged forward and grabbed for the gun, forcing it out of her hand as it fell to the carpet beneath us. She was quick as she tried to escape

my grip on her, scratching and clawing as I tried to pin her in place.
I heard a loud sound as the front door burst open and heavy footsteps
rushed into the room. Cindy and I both reached for the gun at the same
time as I watched muscular arms wrap around her waist and swing her
out of reach. I grabbed the gun and spun around to see Chaz holding
Cindy with her arms bound behind her. Her breathing was heavy as
she tried pulling against him with no luck.

"You okay man?" he asked as he looked me over.

"Yeah, thanks. Get her out of here while I call 911. Don't let her out of
your sight."

I grabbed my phone and waited for the dispatcher to answer while I
ripped off my jacket and held it against Mia's stomach to try to stop
the bleeding.

Forty
Noah

Everything from that point went by in a blur as the paramedics loaded Jade and Mia on stretchers and rushed them away by ambulance. I rode in the ambulance with Jade, watching as they hooked her up to countless devices, trying to keep her alive. I folded my hands together and rested my head on them as my feet tapped anxiously on the floor as the ambulance sped toward the hospital.

Our ambulance pulled up right behind Mia's and I watched as Chase came running toward it, stepping to the side as they brought Mia out and rushed her inside. He ran a hand through his hair and looked up at the gloomy sky before turning his attention to me. A few minutes later they had Jade out of the ambulance and were rushing her inside as well, leaving Chase and I outside in the cold.

"What the fuck happened?!" He demanded as he looked at me, shaking his head.

I rubbed a hand down my face, frustrated that I had been asking myself the same fucking thing.

"Chase-," I started but stopped when the lump in my throat choked the rest of the words from coming out. I looked away and shook my head, embarrassed.

"Stop. Just stop, Noah."

I knew he was pissed, and I didn't blame him. I would be too. If it wasn't for me, his wife wouldn't be in the emergency room, fighting for her life.

"I'm so sorry," I choked out as my voice broke, unable to keep the emotions out.

"Me too." He pulled me into a hug and patted me on the back as I hugged him back. We went inside and checked in with the receptionist at the front desk where we were informed that both girls had been rushed into surgery and we would need to wait in the emergency room waiting area for an update.

We sat in silence for a few minutes before I saw two uniformed cops walk in and stop at the receptionist's desk. She pointed in our direction and they nodded and walked towards us.

"Noah Wilder?" The female cop asked as they stood in front of us.

"That's me." I leaned forward in my chair as they took a seat across from us, pulling out a notepad and pen.

"I'm Officer Perry and this is Officer Daws. We would like to ask you some questions about what happened this morning."

"Okay, whatever you want to know."

The female, Officer Perry, smiled kindly at me as she waited for the other officer to get his notepad ready before she began her questioning. I gave them a quick rundown of everything that had happened leading up to the shooting in Cindy's apartment. I noticed Chase's hands balled into fists as he listened, guilt flooding me for not getting up there sooner. He trusted me to keep her safe and I let him down.

"Thank you for your statement, we'll be back later to speak with Mia and Jade when they are out of surgery." She stood up to leave and I hated the thought that filled my mind. What if they didn't make it out of surgery? I sighed and leaned back against the chair, closing my eyes while I tried to focus on anything other than wondering what was happening in the operating rooms.

"Look, Noah, about what happened," Chase leaned forward and rested his elbows on his knees as he turned his head to look at me. "It's not your fault."

"Bullshit."

"It's not. You had no idea what was going to happen. Regardless of whether we wanted her to go or not, Mia was going to go to that apartment."

"I shouldn't have waited so long to go up there. I should have been right there with her."

"Then you guys would never have been allowed inside. No one would've known that Jade was there." Chase shook his head as he looked down at the floor. "I'm not happy about what happened, not by any means. But I honestly don't think we would have found Jade any other way. Mia saved her life by forcing us to let her do this."

"And it almost cost her hers," I breathed out.

"I know."

I looked over at him and saw the worry etched into his face as he tried to be strong and be a good friend to me. His wife was lying on an operating table while we were stuck doing nothing but praying that she would make it. A few minutes later I watched as the doors to the emergency room flew open and Grant came walking towards us with concern on his face. We stood to give him a quick hug before he sat across from us and looked down the hall.

"Any word yet?" he asked cautiously.

We both shook our heads no. I looked up at him and saw the same sadness I had seen on his face when we were at this very hospital when his wife died. My heart felt like it was about to burst from the mounting pressure.

"Where's Liam?" Chase asked, breaking the silence.

"With mom. He didn't need to come back here for this."

I ran a hand over my shoulder and rubbed the muscles in my neck, trying to get some relief.

"So what happened with Cindy?" Grant leaned back against his chair but didn't fully relax.

"Last I saw Chaz was still practically sitting on her until they got her in handcuffs."

"Chaz?" Grant's eyes went wide when he heard the name.

"Yeah, he actually came in right after the gun went off and held her until the police got there," I recounted as I could hardly believe it myself.

"No shit?" Grant chuckled.

"No shit. Who knew he was actually a decent guy?" I leaned back against the chair and thought about how wrong I was about him and that Jade would have actually been safe living with him after all.

"That's some crazy shit. Chaz is a good guy and Cindy is a psycho. Who would have ever guessed?" Grant asked as he tried to fill the silence between us. I watched as Chase kept his head down while he sent a text message, likely to Mia's dad.

"You're telling me." I shook my head and tapped my foot on the tile floor, desperate for someone to give us an update.

"Did Cindy admit the baby isn't yours?" Grant shifted in his seat, keeping his eyes peeled on the door leading to the emergency room as a doctor lingered near the door, talking to a nurse. There was so much tension between the three of us that none of us could seem to sit still.

"No, she's still insisting that it's mine."

"What are you going to do?"

"Just wait it out I guess? Get the paternity test as soon as the baby is born and if it's mine, I'll fight for full custody. Either way, no child deserves a mother like that."

The doors to the emergency room slid open as the doctor made his way through, pulling off the surgical cap from his head as he walked over to where we were sitting.

"I'm guessing one of you is here for Jade Allyson?" He looked back and forth between us as he sat down. There was no one else in the waiting room.

"That's me," I raised my hand sheepishly, "Is she alright?"

"She's out of surgery and is in recovery right now, we should know more once she's awake." His smile didn't reach his eyes and I knew there was more he wasn't saying.

"Doctor, please. She's the love of my life. Just tell me." I leaned forward as my eyes pleaded with his. He let out a heavy breath and looked around as if he was making sure no one else would hear what he was about to say.

"There's no way to know for sure what her recovery will look like because we don't know how long she was unconscious. She lost a lot of blood and was pretty dehydrated, but thankfully, she didn't have any damage that wasn't repairable. However," his chest fell as sadness filled his tired eyes. "We weren't able to save the pregnancy."

My eyes shot up to his as my brows pulled together in confusion. Grant and Chase whipped their heads over in his direction as well.

"I'm sorry, I don't think I heard you correctly." I leaned closer as I waited for him to repeat himself, to correct what I thought I had heard.

"The pregnancy was no longer viable due to the extent of her injuries. I'm very sorry."

"She was pregnant?"

"It was fairly early, I would say around eight weeks. But definitely pregnant."

I covered my mouth with my hand and leaned back as I felt Chase's hand pat my knee.

"I had no idea."

"I can discuss the loss with her when she's awake. Unfortunately now we just wait for her to come to, then we can see what her recovery will look like."

He shook our hands before walking back to the emergency room, leaving me to sit in stunned silence as Chase sat beside me and Grant across from me. My head was spinning, not knowing that Jade was pregnant, only to find out that she had lost it because of me. Because someone else was so wretched and vile that they would use her to hurt me. I clenched my fists as I worked my jaw, the fury inside me starting to build.

"Let's go for a walk." Chase patted my shoulder as he stood up and led me down the hallway. We stepped outside into the cold air as I turned around and kicked a trash can, releasing some of my anger and frustration in the process. There wasn't much that I knew at that moment other than I would go to my grave making Cindy pay for what she took from me.

Forty One
Jade

The sound of faint talking around me forced me awake. My eyes felt heavy as I struggled to open them, the room overly bright with white walls and fluorescent lights hanging from the ceiling. A few nurses stood beside my bed wearing scrubs while a man in a white lab coat talked to them while looking at something on a clipboard. As I looked around I saw a handful of machines turned on, each making its own noise, which thankfully wasn't any louder than their voices.

I tried to pull myself up into a sitting position, the feel of the tape on my hand pulling against my skin as I saw the needle underneath. A nurse turned to look at me and stepped away from the others as she walked to my bed.

"Did you want to sit up some?" Her voice was soft and friendly, immediately putting me at ease. My throat was sore and felt raw from screaming so I nodded my head yes. She pushed a button on the side of the bed, and I relaxed against the pillow behind me as the bed was adjusted so I could sit up without having to actually try. The other nurse and doctor turned their attention to me, both waiting for me to get situated.

"Hello Jade, I'm Doctor Murphy." He smiled as he sat down on the stool that he pulled out from underneath the counter across from the bed. I tried to give him the best smile I could but stopped when the pain increased. His lips pulled into a thin line as he offered a sympathetic smile in return.

"I'll try to avoid asking you too many questions for now as I know you're probably still feeling a bit weak, however the police will be in shortly to talk with you now that you're awake."

I listened carefully and nodded my head in acknowledgment.

"You had quite a few severe injuries that required surgical intervention, but I'm happy to say that we were able to stop the internal bleeding and everything looks like it should heal just fine. Unfortunately, we weren't able to save the pregnancy." His eyes lowered as he said it and my head tilted to the side in confusion.

"What?" I managed to croak out, the pain worth it if it meant that he repeated what he just said. There was no way I was pregnant. I had been told years ago when I was diagnosed with Polycystic Ovary Syndrome that my chances of getting pregnant would be slim.

"You were pregnant, I would say around eight weeks, however the injuries to your abdominal area were too much for the pregnancy to overcome. I'm so very sorry."

I watched him in disbelief, unable to believe the words he was saying. How did I not know that I was pregnant? My heart dropped as I thought about how devastated Noah would be when he found out. We had never talked in depth about having a family of our own, but we had recently started thinking about it after Cindy showed up. Or at least I had.

He spent the next ten minutes talking to me about recovery and what I could and couldn't do for the next few weeks. Basically, I needed to do as little as possible for the next week while my body tried to heal. While that sounded wonderful, I knew it wasn't realistic given that I had rent to pay and other bills that required that I go to work this week. I tried to keep my anxiety from skyrocketing as he talked, and then again after he left, and I talked with the police about what had happened. I did my best to get the details out without straining my voice too much, and thankfully they were very sympathetic and didn't try to rush me. I was ready for everyone to leave so I could rest. As they were finishing up, they gave me an update on Cindy after I agreed to press charges and confirmed that she would be serving time for attempted murder.

I froze in place as they discussed the shooting and that they didn't have an update on the female victim who was in critical condition. I remembered Mia coming into the room but I blacked out shortly after that and had no idea until right now that she was lying somewhere on an operating table in this hospital, fighting for her life.

Tears slid down my face as they wrapped up their interview and quietly exited the room. A few minutes later I heard another knock on the door and silently groaned that I couldn't get one moment of rest. I watched the door open as Noah peeked his head around the door before coming in. He stepped inside and closed the door quietly behind him, lingering near the foot of the bed as if he wasn't sure whether to come near me.

My heart felt like it was breaking all over again, first for Mia, and now for myself. I hated that Cindy had pushed Noah and I so far apart that he wasn't sure if he was welcome in my hospital room. I lowered my head into my hands as the tears flooded out as I sobbed uncontrollably. I could hear his footsteps as he quickly crossed the room and made his way to my bed, sitting on the side next to me as he wrapped his arms tightly around my shoulders and pulled me into his chest. I turned slightly, afraid to accidentally disconnect one of the many wires that were hooked up to me, and too sore to try to move. He planted soft kisses along the top of my head as he held me and let me cry.

"Shhh, it's okay baby. I've got you, you're safe now," he whispered in my ear.

I felt my body crumble against his and any strength I felt I had left quickly withered away in his arms.

Forty Two
Noah

There were very few moments in my life where I had ever felt as completely helpless as I did now. Holding Jade in my arms as she cried ripped my heart out. I wanted to do whatever I could to make her feel better and yet there was nothing that I could do. She was laying in that hospital bed because of me. Her best friend was fighting for her life, because of me.

I took a break to go give Chase and Grant an update on Jade when the nurses came in to do some additional bloodwork. As I was heading back to the emergency room waiting area, I heard low voices right as I was about to turn the corner. The tone of voice stopped me in my tracks as I recognized it as the voice of Jade's doctor. I stopped to listen.

"I'm so very sorry, we did everything we could. Unfortunately, she did not make it." His voice was even as he delivered the devastating news. I heard crying as he said the words, silence filling the room. A few minutes later a door closed, and the sound of sniffling lingered behind.

I ran a hand down my face before bending over and trying to catch my breath. There was no way this was happening. Mia couldn't be dead. They had to be wrong. There had to be more that they could do. She deserved to live, and her baby girl deserved to have her mother in her life.

I sank down against the wall and sobbed hard into my hands as my body shook with grief.

Forty Three
Jade

After the nurses collected what they needed they went on their way and finally I was left alone to rest for a bit. I wasn't sure when Noah was coming back, but I knew that he was probably busy keeping Chase from going crazy while they waited for an update on Mia. I had tried to ask the nurses if they knew how she was doing but they weren't able to give me that information.

The tv was on with some random cooking show playing as I tried to eat some cold applesauce, hoping it would soothe my throat. I watched as they moved around the kitchen, every move deliberate as they created masterpieces from basic ingredients. The more I watched, the more into the show I got, and part of me was anxious to get out of this room so I could get home and attempt to make something half as fancy as they created.

A little while later they brought a food tray for lunch and I looked at it with a judgmental eye as it was nowhere near as impressive as what I had seen on tv. I pushed the food around the plate with a spoon as I debated whether to try to eat or not. My appetite had yet to return but I knew that if I wanted to have a quicker recovery, I needed to take care of myself. I forced a spoonful of mashed potatoes and gravy into my mouth and worked to swallow and get it down, the pain from my throat making it harder.

Deciding that there was plenty of time to eat later, I pushed the tray away and pressed the button to lower my bed. I adjusted the pillow behind my head and tried to roll over as far as I could on my side, given that I was still hooked up to a handful of machines. Once comfortable I closed my eyes and felt my hand slide down to my stomach. The thought that there had been a baby inside of me tore at my heart as I pressed my hand harder where my baby had died. The tears came rolling down my face as I grieved for a life that I never knew existed until after it was already gone.

A few hours later I woke up to a loud beeping noise and rolled over to see what was happening. I felt dizzy and a little nauseous from the sudden movement and before I knew it a handful of nurses came rushing into my room. I tried to keep my eyes focused on what was happening, but the room started spinning and next thing I knew, everything was black.

Forty Four
Noah

I had been a terrible best friend by avoiding Chase for the last hour after hearing the news about Mia. Maybe I was just selfish or maybe I just couldn't handle the grief on top of the guilt of knowing that her death was my fault. I had walked outside to get some fresh air and the next thing I knew, I had walked a few miles away from the hospital. My mind was chaotic as I tried to figure out how to get past the anger so I could be the friend he needed me to be. But how could I do that when I couldn't even begin to forgive myself.

My pocket buzzed against my thigh as my cell phone vibrated. I pulled it out and saw Grant's name on the caller ID.

"Hey," I answered as I ran a hand through my hair.

"Where are you?" His tone was hard, and I knew he was mad.

"I went for a walk."

"Well get your ass back here now. Jade was just rushed back into the OR, she had a complication from surgery."

He hung up before I could ask anything more. I shoved my phone back into my pocket and took off running as fast as I could. Once I made it back to the hospital, I went flying through the doors to the emergency room, scanning the room for the receptionist who was supposed to be at the front desk. I slammed my hands on the desk in frustration before I felt a hand on my shoulder and spun around.

Grant eyed me cautiously as he took a step back and put his hands up in front of him.

"You okay?" he asked with concern.

"Where is she? Is there an update?"

"The doctor just came out and said that she had started bleeding again, but they were able to find it and stop it. She's going to be okay."

His words calmed me as I felt my heart pound in my chest. I looked into the waiting room and found Chase sitting there with his head in his hands. In my rush to get back to Jade, I had forgotten that I also needed to get back to him. I patted Grant on the shoulder as I smiled and walked over to Chase.

I sat in the chair next to him and patted his back in an attempt to comfort him.

"I'm so sorry, man. I should have been here when you got the news. I just, I couldn't handle it, and I left. And I know, it was a dick move and I'm sorry. I feel terrible and I don't expect you to ever forgive me."

He slightly turned his head and looked up at me, his eyebrows pulled together in confusion.

"What the fuck are you talking about?"

"Mia. I heard the doctor giving you the update as I was coming back from Jade's room. I'm so sorry, I don't even know where to begin. Have you told Joe and Arlene yet?" My mind started to wander as I thought about all of the people we needed to tell, the arrangements that needed to be made. There was a lot that needed to be done.

"Again, what are you talking about?" He gave me the oddest look as he pulled back and leaned against the back of the chair and watched me. Grant stood across from us, leaning against the wall, giving me the same odd look.

"I'm talking about Mia! What the fuck is wrong with you guys? She's dead and you're acting like nothing fucking happened?!" I was about to lose my mind.

"Mia's not dead," Grant said from across the room. My head turned in his direction, one eyebrow raised.

"What?" I was beyond confused, I knew what I had heard.

"Mia's not dead," Chase said and watched me. "Why would you think that she was?"

"Because I heard the doctor when I was coming back. I stopped before I came around the corner and heard him saying that they did everything they could and that they weren't able to save her," I explained as I looked back and forth between them.

"So you just assumed it was Mia?" Chase was still giving me a look like he thought I had lost my mind.

"There was no one else in the waiting room when I left, so yeah, I thought it was Mia."

"Another family came in right after you went to see Jade. A woman who had been in a rollover car accident. She died within minutes of them trying to operate. That's who you heard the doctor talking about."

I put my face in my hands and shook my head, both frustrated and embarrassed.

"Okay, so do you have an update on Mia?"

"The doctor came out a little while ago and confirmed that everything went well with her surgery. The bullet missed any organs and had a clean exit. She's in recovery and they'll let us know when she can have visitors, but she's going to be fine," Chase said with a smile.

"So then everyone is okay?" I asked, still not believing it. Grant and Chase chuckled as they watched me, the guy who always had it together was a literal hot mess.

"Yeah, everyone is going to be just fine," Grant assured me from across the room. I let out the breath I felt like I had been holding all day and sunk down lower in my chair as I waited for another update.

Forty Five
Jade

The next few days passed by relatively quickly and before I knew it, I was being released from the hospital. I packed up the few things I had with me and sat on the edge of the bed while I waited for the nurse to hand me the discharge paperwork to sign. My fingers gripped the pen harder than what was needed as I scribbled across the papers. The relief of being able to go home and not have to deal with Cindy felt so nice, almost unbelievable.

As the nurse smiled and walked out the door, I saw Noah pop in behind her, a bouquet of roses in his hand as he walked toward my bed. I smiled back at him, genuinely happy to see him.

"Beautiful roses for a beautiful lady." He held the flowers out for me to take, a tingle spreading across my skin as our hands touched. I nervously reached up to tuck my hair behind my ear when I remembered the mess Cindy had made of my hair. I tucked my head into my chest, embarrassed to have anyone see me this way.

"Thank you, but I'm far from beautiful," I mumbled as I held the bouquet close to my chest.

Noah's finger gently reached beneath my chin and slowly lifted my head as his eyes locked onto mine.

"You are gorgeous," he tried to assure me as I fought to look away.

"Jade, look at me." His voice was soft as he sat down next to me on the bed. "There's not a damn thing that you could do to yourself that would ever make me think you were any less beautiful than what you are. I love every single thing about you."

"What about the things other people do to me?" I winced when his eyes moved from my face to my hair.

"You're still the most beautiful woman I've ever seen. You could be bald, and you'd still be beautiful. Believe it or not, I'm not in love with your hair." He chewed his lip to keep from laughing.

"You seemed to love it when you had your hands wrapped up in it every time we had sex. Now what are you going to do?" I smirked, loving that we were finally getting back to our normal, playful selves.

"Well," he let out an exaggerated sigh as he shrugged his shoulders. "I guess I'll just have to find something else to hold on to. These might do," he joked as he reached across and cupped my breasts. I rolled my eyes as I playfully swatted at him.

"You ready to go?" he asked, bringing my attention back to the fact that I had been discharged yet I was still willingly hanging out in the hospital.

"Yeah, I'm definitely ready to get out of here." I stood up slowly, making sure I didn't lose my balance again before I trusted my body's strength. A lot had improved over the last few days, but I still wasn't anywhere near where I was before having two surgeries back to back.

"Do you think you could give me a ride?" I asked once I had myself situated.

"You know, I was thinking about that," he paused and studied my face. "Instead of taking you back to your apartment, why don't you come stay with me?"

"I don't know if that's such a good idea." There was a hesitation in my voice, and I hated it. Why was I still so reluctant to want to stay with him?

"Okay, I won't push. Just thought I would ask." He pulled his lips together into a tight smile as he stepped to the side and held his hand out for me to walk by.

"I'm sorry, Noah," I said as we walked out into the hallway.

"Don't be, it's fine."

Except everything about his tone and body language told me that it wasn't. It wasn't a big surprise that Noah didn't stay long after he got me back to my apartment. Once I was inside and situated, he talked with Chaz for a few minutes before making up an excuse to leave. My mind raced as I tried to replay everything that had happened over the past few months, desperate to figure out why I was pushing so hard against staying with Noah.

Then it came to me. Before, I had Cindy and the baby to blame for not wanting to get too close to Noah. It was easy when I could say that I was walking away to give Noah a chance to be the dad he wanted to be. To allow them the chance to be the family they should be. But now that Cindy and the baby weren't in the picture the way they had been, I didn't have anything else to focus on. I realized that all along I was the one who was scared to take that next step. Because it wasn't just a step. It was a leap. And fuck if I weren't about to fall.

THE CRADLE WILL FALL

Forty Six
Noah

In the blink of an eye, two weeks had passed, and we were all trying to figure out our new normal after everything that happened with Cindy. I had spent more time at my lawyer's office putting together the paperwork that would be needed once the baby was born, assuming that somehow it ended up being mine. After reaching out to the doctor's office they confirmed that they did receive records from the other clinic Cindy had been seen at, but due to privacy restrictions, they couldn't discuss those results with me.

It felt like I was in a constant state of anxiety as I waited for Cindy's due date to get closer so I could get confirmation on whether or not I was the father. The only thing that put me at ease was knowing that she was locked up and couldn't hurt anyone else. In an effort to give Jade some space, I had been trying to make myself helpful with getting Chase and Mia back on their feet but every time I saw her struggle to hold the baby or wince in pain, it broke my heart. I hated that I was the reason she had to go through all of this.

I stepped outside into the bitter cold as I walked to my truck. It was the beginning of March and while spring would officially be here in a few weeks, that didn't mean shit in Colorado. I pulled my beanie down lower to cover my ears as a chilly wind whipped past me. A few minutes later I was in my truck, free from the wind but not spared from the cold. I quickly started the engine and drove off, heading for Grant's house.

As I pulled up, I noticed Chase's truck parked in the driveway and Jade's car parked in the street. My hands started sweating as I thought about seeing Jade. I wanted things to go back to normal between us but unfortunately, they hadn't. The more time she spent with Chaz, the less time we spent together. I felt an overwhelming amount of jealousy as I watched them sitting together on the couch as I walked in, laughing at something he had said. I looked away as I walked off into the kitchen and found Grant sitting at the kitchen table across from Chase and Mia. I smiled awkwardly as I held out a wrapped gift, waiting for Grant to take it.

"Happy birthday," I said as he pulled me into a quick hug and thanked me. He sat the gift on the counter behind me with the other gifts people had brought. I looked around, quickly scanning the room after noticing Chaz sitting by himself on the couch. I felt eyes burning into my head as I looked down and caught Mia smiling at me.

"I'm pretty sure she just went to the bathroom," she said as she nodded to where Jade had been sitting.

"Who?" I asked dumbly. I was a nervous wreck and it showed. I heard her laugh quietly under her breath as she turned her attention back to Chase as he whispered something in her ear that made her giggle. I walked over to the fridge and held the door open as I looked inside at the beer options. As I was debating between the three options available, I felt someone move behind me. In an instant, I recognized the light floral scent and felt the pull in my chest as I tried to breathe. I turned around and found Jade standing behind me, her thumbs tucked loosely in the front pockets of her skinny jeans.

"Hey," she said as she smiled at me, new happiness in her eyes.

"Hey," I whispered. I took a minute to stop and look at her, to really take her in. Since the last time I saw her, she had colored her hair. It was now a dark brown with subtle highlights streaked through it. There were soft layers that framed her face and the back had been cut short again, similar to how she had worn it when she first moved here. I found myself staring when I heard her giggle and tug at my shirt sleeve.

"You okay over there?" she teased, bringing my attention back to her.

"Yeah, I was just taking in your new look."

"Do you like it?" she asked as she ran a hand up to her hair and tugged at a stray piece, pulling it back behind her ear.

"I do, it looks good on you."

"Thanks." She looked so nervous and uncertain of herself which killed me when I remembered how much confidence she had when we first met.

"Did you find time to go to a salon?" I asked, making random conversation.

"Actually, Chaz did it." Her eyes lit up when she said his name and I felt my stomach drop. It felt like someone had hit me with a bowling ball.

"Chaz?"

I had given him credit for being a good guy with the whole Cindy situation, but helping Jade cut and color her hair seemed a little over the top. Even for him.

"Yeah, it turns out that he's actually going to school for cosmetology. He offered to help, and I let him."

"That was nice of him, I'm glad you guys are getting along so well." I kept my tone even and void of any emotion as I grabbed the bottle opener and opened my beer. I took a long drink, allowing the cold fluid to attempt to cool off the anger I could feel rising from my jealousy.

"He's actually been a great roommate."

As much as I loved hearing the enthusiasm in her voice, it killed me that it was all for Chaz. I took another drink from my bottle as I tried to keep from saying anything stupid.

"That's great, I'm happy for you. I'm gonna go mingle, it was nice to see you." I pushed away from the counter and started to walk past her when I felt her hand wrap around my arm and pull me back.

"Noah," she sighed. "Can we talk? Please?"

"Honestly, Jade, I don't know what else there is to say. I've been trying to talk to you for weeks, but you haven't wanted to listen. Maybe it's best if we just stopped. You have Chaz, and from what I can tell, he's making you happy. Isn't that what really matters?"

"Chaz is gay," she blurted out and my head spun around to look at her, to wait for her to burst into laughter at the joke she just told.

"What are you talking about? He's far from gay."

"I hate to break it to you, but you're wrong." She folded her arms across her chest and leaned back against the counter where I had been standing.

I pulled my eyebrows together in confusion as I thought about what she said. There was absolutely no way he was gay when we had fought each other throughout high school on who could get with the most girls.

"I think there's been a misunderstanding, you must've heard him wrong."

"See for yourself." She nodded behind me and I turned to find Chaz lingering in the doorway, talking to Chase and Mia. As I looked down, I saw him holding someone's hand, but I couldn't see who it was because they were on the other side of the wall. A few seconds later a body turned around and my jaw dropped open when I saw Joey, the bartender from Malarkey's. He wrapped an arm around Chaz as they said their goodbyes and walked out the door.

"No fucking way," I said more to myself than anyone else. I turned back to look at Jade as her eyes danced wildly as they watched my reaction.

"Told you." She pursed her lips together and immediately I wanted to grab them and kiss them.

"Okay, so you were right. Apparently, Chaz is into men. But that still doesn't change things between us. I wanted this to work between us more than I have ever wanted anything else in my life, but this feels too complicated, Jade. Every step forward we take, we end up getting knocked back five." I looked away and shook my head in frustration.

Out of the corner of my eye I watched as Jade leaned down, getting down on one knee as she watched me. I turned and stared at her, not believing my eyes.

"Life is hard, Noah. There's no guarantee that we are meant to be together nor is there a guarantee that we'll have a happily ever after. We're going to have hard times and battles that we won't want to fight. We're going to be pushed to limits that we didn't know we had. But at the end of the day, you're the only one that I want to go through all of this with. The good times, the bad times. All of it. Together." She let out a loud sigh as she quickly glanced around the room at the handful of people who had made their way in to watch.

"I know you wanted to do this first and I'm sorry we didn't get the chance. But I couldn't wait around and hope that you might want to do it again, so I'm gonna do it myself. Noah Wilder, will you marry me?"

I swallowed hard as I sat my beer bottle on the counter behind me before reaching down and helping Jade up. I held her hands in mine as I stared into her eyes, watching the anxiety build as she waited for my answer.

"Fuck yeah, I'll marry you," I growled before I pulled her into me, crushing my mouth down on top of hers. I could feel the heat from her body as it touched mine and wished that no one else was around so I could do what we really wanted to do. I could feel her giggle as the crowd erupted in cheers as I pulled her up and she wrapped her legs around my waist. I held our kiss as long as I could and soon heard the room get quiet as people walked out and joked about us getting a room.

I slowly helped her to her feet as her legs fell from my side and slid to the floor. She smiled up at me and cupped my cheek with her hand. To think that I was so ready to give up and call it quits five minutes ago and now here I was standing in front of my fiancé. While I would have loved to have been the one to propose to her, I loved that she was the one to ask me. If there was ever any doubt about how she felt about us, it was removed the second she asked me to marry her.

"You sure you wanna marry a guy like me?" I smiled as I pulled her hand into mine and brought it up to my lips to kiss it.

"You bet your ass I do. Are you sure you wanna marry a girl like me? I don't have that big, fancy job anymore. Now I wear a uniform and smell like greasy food..." She raised an eyebrow as she smirked.

"It's okay, I've been known to have some food fetishes, I think we can make it work." I winked as she playfully swatted my shoulder. I wrapped my arm around her waist and pulled her into me, bringing her closer for another kiss.

"So does this mean that you're finally going to move in with me?" I joked, hoping it wasn't too much of a sore subject.

"I guess it does." She pulled back and wrapped her arms behind my neck as she looked deep into my eyes. "But I'm still holding you to those four orgasms per day."

I let out a chuckle as I clicked my tongue against the back of my teeth.

"Well, lucky for you, the fiancé package just got upgraded to FIVE per day." I pulled her closer letting my groin line up perfectly so she could feel the bulge that was starting to form in my jeans.

"In that case, is there another upgrade once we're married?" she teased as she rocked her hips forward against me.

"You're gonna be the death of me, woman," I growled as I nipped at her neck, causing her to squeal and try to squirm away.

Epilogue
Noah
3 Months Later

I sat next to Jade on the old wooden bench seat as our hands wrapped together as we waited for the judge to come in. I looked across the small courtroom and stared at Cindy as she sat at the table next to her state-assigned lawyer. Behind them stood a guard ready to strap the handcuffs back on her if she got any ideas. She looked over her shoulder and glared at Jade and I before turning her attention back to the front of the room. Being a total dick, I lifted Jade's hand and brought it to my mouth for a kiss, making sure her diamond engagement ring was in plain sight for Cindy to see. I didn't have to wonder if she saw the ring after she turned her head around and slammed her fist down on the table, forcing the guard to step forward while keeping one hand on his gun that was holstered.

I checked my watch after getting a glance from my lawyer to get my ass up to the table before the judge came in. I kissed Jade quickly on the cheek as I slid out and walked up front to sit where I was supposed to. A few minutes later we all rose as the judge walked in and sat down. I held my breath as I waited for the news that had been tormenting me for the past few months.

As we sat down I felt a hand clasp my shoulder and looked back to see Chase smiling at me as he gave me a reassuring nod. Mia sat beside him with Grant sitting on her other side. There's never been a doubt about how many people I had in my life who would be there to support me and today they were all lined up behind me. I let go of the breath I was holding and sucked in another one as the judge began to speak.

"I see here that this is a court-ordered paternity test and we're reading the official results. Is that correct?" She slid her glasses down her nose and looked back and forth between the two lawyers.

"Yes, your Honor, that is correct." My lawyer sat back down next to me as we waited for her to continue.

"Well then, let's get to it," she said quietly as she read through the report before reading it out loud. "Based on the DNA sample collected from Noah Wilder, this test confirms that you are not the father of the child in question."

I felt the air rush out of me as I leaned forward and shook my head in relief. A few hands patted my back quickly before the judge continued. I heard random chatter around me as the judge wrapped up and went on her way. I turned around and found Jade grinning ear to ear as she leaned over the half wall to hug me.

"It's finally over, baby," I whispered in her ear.

"I'm so happy, now we can finally have our happily ever after." She held onto me as if nothing else mattered. And at that moment, it didn't.

Thirty minutes later I was sliding into the seat next to Jade at SlowMo's. Everyone decided a celebratory lunch was in order after finding out that Cindy would no longer be a part of my life. Deep down I felt heartbroken for the baby, having Cindy for a mother and not knowing its father. I took comfort knowing that he was being cared for by one of the most amazing families in town until they figured out the next steps.

I looked around the table and smiled as I watched the people who had become my family sit and talk with each other. Everything felt so calm and back to normal. Jade was offered another position at the bank after Cindy was arrested. After a very long and overdue apology, Jade happily accepted the position of branch manager at a higher rate than she had been at when they fired her. She was happy to be doing the job she loved with the people she enjoyed working with.

Living together had been easy and seamless as she moved in right after we got engaged, like the very next day. Chaz agreed to continue her lease and ended up asking his boyfriend to move in with him after Jade moved out. It still blew my mind to hear that he had a boyfriend. After quite a few rounds of beer one night, he finally came clean to us and admitted that he had known since high school but was scared to tell anyone. So he made up stories of the girls he had supposedly been with, dealing with the consequences of getting a bad reputation instead of just coming clean.

I looked across the table and smiled at Mia as she held Rylee, letting her play with her necklace. Rylee looked just like Mia and my heart skipped a beat every time I thought about what could have happened if the bullet would have been a fraction of an inch over. There wouldn't be a beautiful mother to compare this sweet baby to.

Jade's laughter next to me pulled me back into the conversation as she teased Grant about making the moves on the new waitress at SlowMo's. Her eyes lit up as she watched him blush when the waitress headed towards the table. Her fingers gently slid the locket around the chain, moving it back to where it should be. By her heart. I hadn't seen Jade take the locket off once since she got it back, a constant smile on her face every time she touched it.

The waitress leaned across Grant, placing the glasses of water in front of us. She smiled down at him before turning her attention to Liam.

"Need anything else, Champ?" she asked, casting a glance back at Grant.

"Nope." His answer was short as he kept his attention focused on the ketchup bottle as he tapped his palm against it, flinging bits of ketchup across his plate.

"What's the deal?" I asked as I nodded toward the waitress after she walked off.

"Nothing." He shook his head and looked down at Liam. The waitress made her way back up to the register and smiled at Grant as she looked over at our table again.

"You sure about that?" I chuckled.

"Yeah, we're good. Summer break just started so we don't need any distractions." There was a sadness in his tone and I made a note to try to pull him aside soon to talk to him. I knew that he was more open to the idea of trying to date again, but from the looks of it, Liam wasn't ready for him to move on from Renee.

After we finished eating, we said our goodbyes and climbed into the truck. I was about to head back to our house, it felt so fucking weird to say that, but had another idea at the last minute. Jade sat quietly next to me the entire ride, holding my hand as it rested on the middle console. Her window was rolled down as she held her arm out and let the warm breeze caress it as we drove down the deserted back road.

I pulled the truck over to the side of the road, under the big old tree that I loved coming here for. We hopped out of the truck and I held out my hand to help her climb up into the bed. I quickly reached into the backseat and grabbed the blankets I kept back there for this exact reason. I quietly closed the door and jumped into the bed of the truck, helping her lay the blankets down before we got comfy.

I leaned back against the window of the cab and pulled her into me. Her body felt so soft and fragile against mine, a constant reminder for me of what she had been through. Also, a constant reminder of how strong she really was. I heard her yawn as her body sank lower, knowing she was exhausted from our late night last night.

"You want me to take you home so you can rest?" I offered as I leaned to the side to look at her.

"I'm good here. I like the fresh air and quietness."

"Me too," I whispered in her ear.

"But we can't fall asleep out here, and if we get too comfortable, we're definitely going to fall asleep," I warned.

Her head tilted to the side as she turned to look at me.

"Are you worried about having another bad dream?" Her voice was filled with concern as I felt my body get tense as she brought it up. I hadn't had a nightmare about Jade since she got out of the hospital. It felt like once Cindy was locked up and Jade asked me to marry her, everything just sort of stopped. No more bad dreams. No more doubt or insecurities about our relationship.

But hearing Jade ask about them made my body react the same way it did when I would have a bad dream and I realized that it was because those nightmares almost came true. The dreams of Cindy holding Jade hostage and trying to take her from me- that was a fucking reality. And now it would forever be a living nightmare.

I forced a smile as I looked down at her and tried to force the tension out of my voice when I spoke.

"No baby, I don't worry about bad dreams anymore. Those are gone now that I have you." I watched as her eyes lit up as she smiled back at me. "However, this is bear country and unless you want to be a snack, we shouldn't be getting too comfortable out here."

"Got it. We don't want the bears to eat me." She giggled as she pressed further against my chest.

"Exactly. That's my job." I tickled her sides as I made snarling sounds against her neck, enjoying the sound of her laughter as it floated around us.

The drive back to the house was quiet, the soft sound of Jade snoring filling the cab. I drove slowly and took my time, making sure to avoid going too fast on the rugged roads so it didn't wake her. Every time I looked over at her, her face looked so peaceful but all I could see was the woman who had laid on the floor in front of me and almost died.

My hand tightened around the steering wheel as I tried to force the thought out of my head. Even though Jade and I had come so far in our relationship over the past few months I still couldn't get past the guilt that ate away at me knowing that her life had been put on the line because of me. No matter how much I tried to force the thoughts away, they always sat right there in the front of my mind, reminding me of how much I didn't deserve her.

An hour later and I had run out of back roads to take so I decided to head home. I waited for the garage door to finish opening, the loud creaking sound waking Jade up in the process. She yawned as she looked around then smiled at me.

"Why did you let me sleep the whole way home?"

"You looked like you needed it," I said as I hopped out of the truck and walked around to her side to help her out.

"I'm not a delicate flower anymore, Noah, the doctor said I was fully recovered. Remember?"

I opened the door leading into the house and stood to the side to let her go first.

"I know but I'm a firm believer in the idea that if you're tired, you should sleep." I shrugged my shoulders and winked at her as I walked past her to go into the kitchen. The truth was that I wanted her to sleep because regardless of what the doctor had said, I knew Jade and I knew she wasn't back to herself yet. She got tired too often and too easily the past few weeks and I was damn sure going to make sure she was getting the rest she needed.

I glanced over my shoulder and smiled when I saw her curl up on the couch and cuddle into her favorite throw blanket. It was the start of summer but that didn't mean she didn't like to cuddle her blankets. She pulled it up under her chin and bent her knees up to her chest as she rested her head on them. The light filtered in through the window, casting a warm glow on her beautiful face.

"So, what do you want for dinner?" I asked as I held the refrigerator door open and looked inside. "I can grill burgers, or we have a frozen pizza that I can toss in the oven."

"Fix whatever sounds good to you, I don't know if I'll eat." Her eyes watched mine as she said it, knowing that I wouldn't be happy about her not eating.

"Why not?" I closed the door and walked over to sit next to her on the couch.

"I just don't feel like it. I'm a little nauseous."

"Hmmm, you're nauseous and tired. Maybe you're pregnant?" There was more hope in my voice than I had wanted and I instantly regretted it when I saw her eyes drop and look down at the floor.

"You know I'm not pregnant."

"You could be. It happened once, you never know, it could happen again." My voice was soft and gentle as I placed a hand on her knee.

"That was a once in a lifetime thing Noah, you know that. You were there when we talked to the doctor. The chance of me getting pregnant again is slim to none. And the chance of me being able to carry the baby to term would be even less. It would take a miracle."

Her eyes filled with tears and I felt terrible for making her talk about this again. She was right, I had been there with her at the doctor's when they had told her she was unlikely to get pregnant again. It felt as soul-crushing now as it did then. But part of me couldn't give up on the idea that we were meant to be parents. That she was meant to be the mother to my children. That feeling gnawed at me the same way the guilt did. Soon there wouldn't be anything left.

I leaned forward and pulled her into me, holding her as I heard her sniffle. Her chest fell heavily as she tried to stop the tears that I had caused.

"I'm sorry Jade, I shouldn't have said that. I didn't mean to upset you."

"It's not your fault for wanting something that I can't give you," she whispered.

I leaned to the side to make sure she could see me before I started talking. Gently I reached over and held her chin between my fingers as I turned her face to look up at me.

"Jade, you give me everything I could ever want or need. There's not a single thing that I could want that you're not giving me. Who knows what our future holds, but just because we may not get our miracle baby, that doesn't mean that we can't have our own family. We can make this into whatever we want, and as long as you're in my life, I know it will be beautiful."

I felt my heart pull deep inside my chest as she reached up and cupped my cheek before pulling my face down to kiss her. It was at that moment that I realized that the things we considered to be our imperfections weren't the things that actually defined us. The things that I thought we needed to make us happy no longer mattered. She was all that I needed to make me happy, and I finally had her.

Other Books By Samantha Baca

The Haven Brook Series:
’Til Death Do Us Part (Haven Brook Book 1)
https://books2read.com/u/m2RJNR

The Cradle Will Fall (Haven Brook Book 2)
https://books2read.com/u/b6O0QE

The Ties That Bind (Haven Brook Book 3)
https://books2read.com/u/mqgoz8

A Very Haven Christmas (Haven Brook Book 4- Novella)
https://books2read.com/u/mvqGjj

Three Strikes, You’re Gone (Haven Brook Book 5)
https://books2read.com/u/mvqL2z

The Dark Shadows Series
Five Steps Ahead (Dark Shadows Book 1)
https://books2read.com/u/38Q0gO

Ten Seconds Too Late (Dark Shadows Book 2)
Coming 2022

Against The Clock (Dark Shadows Book 3)
Coming 2022

Out Of Time (Dark Shadows Book 4)
Coming 2023

The Stone Creek Series (Novellas)
Chocolate Covered Mistletoe (Stone Creek Book 1)
https://books2read.com/u/3LRk9N

Candy Coated Promises (Stone Creek Book 2)
https://books2read.com/u/mldP5Y

Pumpkin Spiced Possibilities (Stone Creek Book 3)
https://books2read.com/u/bojdwV

Stand-Alone Books
One Last Wish
https://books2read.com/u/mqg7D9

Finding Love In Apartment 2C (Novella)
https://books2read.com/u/bze9aZ

Acknowledgements

First and foremost, I want to thank the voices in my head that kept me up late at night and tripled my dependency on caffeine as they forced this book to come to life while I was trying to sleep. Apparently, Noah and Jade are quite the night owls and had a lot to say.

To my wonderful, loving, and incredibly talented husband, Richard- thank you for being a fucking superhero. From plotting ideas to proofreading and cover designs, you never stopped busting your ass to make this book what I wanted it to be. Between writing snacks and fueling me up with plenty of coffee, you helped me crank this book out and I enjoyed every second of it. Thank you for helping make another dream come true for me. I've said it before and I'll say it again, I will always be eternally grateful for everything you do for me.

Chelsea, your love for books flows into your love of helping me write mine and it fills my heart with so much happiness. I love how dedicated and invested you are in helping me, and how we can talk about anything. When I'm stuck on an idea and have no idea where to go with it, you jump right in and help me navigate, making it feel easier and less overwhelming. When I have new book ideas or other exciting news, you jump right in and share my excitement. I'm so thankful to have you on my alpha team and I will cut anyone who tries to steal you away. CUT them...

Azucena, if someone would have told me in middle school that we would share all of the experiences that we've been through together, I would have thought they were crazy. You have been by my side through all of my crazy adventures and different hobbies, and now I've turned you into a romance reader! It completely warms my heart when I get a text message or phone call from you, checking to make sure you have the current manuscript. Your dedication to me and this process is incredible and I'm so grateful for it. I can't imagine doing this with anyone else. And like with Chelsea, if anyone tries to steal you away from me, I will cut them as well...

Debi, you are always one of the first to volunteer to beta read for me and I love that you help me with proofreading as well. I love our friendship and it makes me so happy to see us continue on throughout the years and through different adventures. Thank you for helping make my dreams a reality.

Amanda, I still remember asking a question in a Facebook group about paternity tests and you jumping in to confirm that you didn't have the answer but that you needed to read this book! I'm so thankful that we connected and started the friendship that we have. Your love for reading has helped me tremendously by making sure that my writing stays on track and that I deliver a book that readers will enjoy. Thank you for taking the time to proofread this for me as well, I always appreciate the feedback.

Jennifer, it's hard to believe that we have known each other all our lives and that no matter where the road leads, it never separates us. I love that you're in this chapter of my life with me, jumping in and reading my books while helping me to make sure I haven't missed anything. I rely on you to give me feedback as a reader and you never let me down. Thank you for always being so supportive, it really means a lot to me.

Tillie, I have enjoyed working with you as you helped me with edits and gave me feedback. My favorite part was the late night text messages when you got to the good parts that inevitably kept you up late because you HAD to finish. You've been incredibly helpful, and I can't imagine not having you on my team!

Katie, thank you for being so eager to get your hands on the next book and for taking the time out of your busy schedule to read them for me. I appreciate the love and support that you have shown and continue to show me on this journey. Maybe someday we can create our own version of The Vine where we can hangout, relax, and enjoy some drinks!

To my parents and sister, thank you for continuing to believe in me and for your words of encouragement as I keep setting new goals and pushing myself to go further. I love the confidence you have in me that if I put my mind to it, I'll be able to do it. You guys are the best support system and cutest cheerleaders I could I ever ask for.

My dear, sweet girls, I continue to push harder and work through the struggles to show you later that anything is possible if you just put your mind to it. I have so much love for you and can't wait to see what you do with this beautiful life you've been given.

I would like to thank all of the readers who took the time to read Noah and Jade's story, I hope you enjoyed it. Thank you to everyone who has read everything I've written, including my silly posts on Facebook and Instagram, it feels AMAZING to have so many new friends! I hope you'll continue to follow me through this journey and that you love each new book a little more than the one before. Thank you for taking a chance on me.

About the Author

Samantha lives in the southwest with her husband and two small children after abandoning her childhood dream of living in a cabin in Colorado when she found that she couldn't afford to live there and was deathly allergic to the woods. When she's not writing she's usually spouting off sarcastic remarks while drinking wine out of a coffee mug to look like a functional adult while chasing down her toddlers. She enjoys spending time with her family, watching reruns of FRIENDS, and the 24/7 flow of coffee that can be found in her veins. Be sure to follow her on social media for updates on what she's working on.

You can find her here:

Facebook: https://www.facebook.com/AuthorSamanthaBaca

Instagram: https://instagram.com/author_samantha_baca

Goodreads: http://www.goodreads.com/authorsamanthabaca

Facebook Reader Group:
https://www.facebook.com/groups/2945710968775398/

Webpage: https://authorsamanthabaca.wordpress.com

Newsletter: http://eepurl.com/g0NcSj